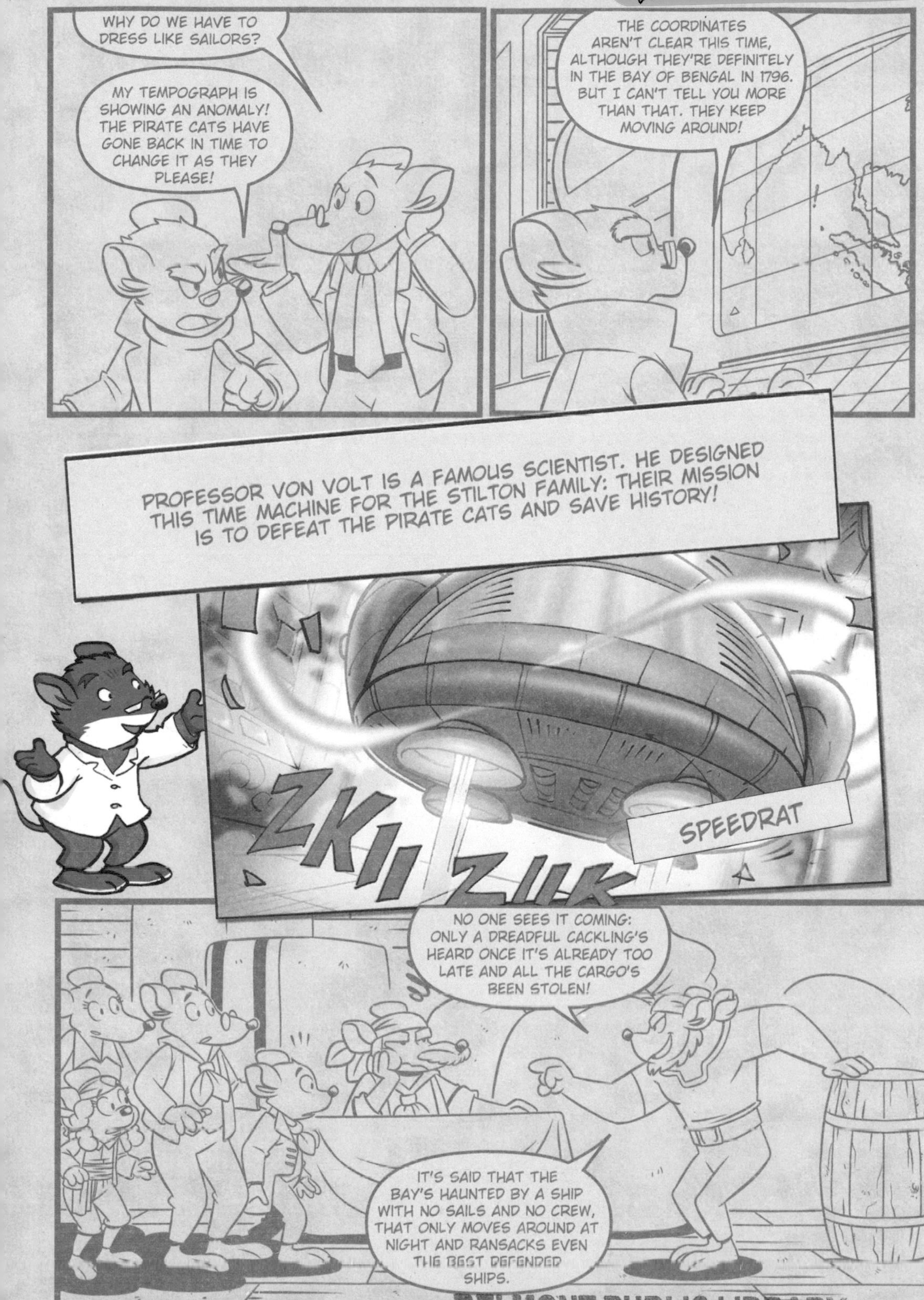
WHY DO WE HAVE TO DRESS LIKE SAILORS?
MY TEMPOGRAPH IS SHOWING AN ANOMALY! THE PIRATE CATS HAVE GONE BACK IN TIME TO CHANGE IT AS THEY PLEASE!
THE COORDINATES AREN'T CLEAR THIS TIME, ALTHOUGH THEY'RE DEFINITELY IN THE BAY OF BENGAL IN 1796. BUT I CAN'T TELL YOU MORE THAN THAT. THEY KEEP MOVING AROUND!
PROFESSOR VON VOLT IS A FAMOUS SCIENTIST. HE DESIGNED THIS TIME MACHINE FOR THE STILTON FAMILY: THEIR MISSION IS TO DEFEAT THE PIRATE CATS AND SAVE HISTORY!
ZKII
SPEEDRAT
NO ONE SEES IT COMING: ONLY A DREADFUL CACKLING'S HEARD ONCE IT'S ALREADY TOO LATE AND ALL THE CARGO'S BEEN STOLEN!
IT'S SAID THAT THE BAY'S HAUNTED BY A SHIP WITH NO SAILS AND NO CREW, THAT ONLY MOVES AROUND AT NIGHT AND RANSACKS EVEN THE BEST DEFENDED SHIPS.

Geronimo Stilton

PAPERCUTZ™

Geronimo Stilton & Thea Stilton

GRAPHIC NOVELS AVAILABLE FROM PAPERCUTZ

...ALSO AVAILABLE WHEREVER E-BOOKS ARE SOLD!

#1
"The Discovery
of America"

#2
"The Secret
of the Sphinx"

#3
"The Coliseum
Con"

#4
"Following the
Trail of Marco Polo"

#5
"The Great
Ice Age"

#6
"Who Stole
The Mona Lisa?"

#7
"Dinosaurs
in Action"

#8
"Play It Again,
Mozart!"

#9
"The Weird
Book Machine"

#10
"Geronimo Stilton
Saves the Olympics"

#11
"We'll Always
Have Paris"

#12
"The First Samurai"

#13
"The Fastest Train
in the West"

#14
"The First Mouse
on the Moon"

#15
"All for Stilton,
Stilton for All!"

#16
"Lights, Camera,
Stilton!"

#17
"The Mystery of the
Pirate Ship"

#1
"The Secret
of Whale Island"

#2
"Revenge of
the Lizard Club"

#3
"The Treasure of
the Viking Ship"

#4
"Catching the
Giant Wave"

#5
"The Secret of the
Waterfall in the Woods"

papercutz.com

Geronimo Stilton

THE MYSTERY OF THE PIRATE SHIP

By Geronimo Stilton

NEW YORK

J
FIC
STI
GRAPHIC

GERONIMO STILTON #17
THE MYSTERY OF THE PIRATE SHIP

Geronimo Stilton names, characters and related indicia are copyright, trademark and exclusive license of Atlantyca S.p.A.
All rights reserved.
The moral right of the author has been asserted.

Text by Geronimo Stilton
Cover by Ryan Jampole (artist) and JayJay Jackson (colorist)
Editorial supervision by Alessandra Berello (Atlantyca S.p.A.)
Script by Francesco Savino and Leonardo Favia
Translation by Nanette McGuinness
Art by Ryan Jampole
Color by Matt Herms and Laurie E. Smith
Lettering by Wilson Ramos Jr.

© Atlantyca S.p.A. – via Leopardi 8, 20123 Milano, Italia – foreignrights@atlantyca.it
© 2016 for this Work in English language by Papercutz, 160 Broadway, Suite 700, East Wing, New York, NY 10038

Based on an original idea by Elisabetta Dami

www.geronimostilton.com

Stilton is the name of a famous English cheese. It is a registered trademark of the Stilton Cheese Makers' Association.
For more information go to www.stiltoncheese.com

Production – Dawn Guzzo
Production Coordinator – Jeff Whitman
Editor – Carol M. Burrell
Associate Editor – Bethany Bryan
Jim Salicrup
Editor-in-Chief

ISBN: 978-1-62991-451-0

Printed in China.
April 2016 by WKT Co. LTD.
3/F Phase 1 Leader Industrial Centre
188 Texaco Road, Tsuen Wan, N.T.
Hong Kong

Papercutz books may be purchased for business or promotional use.
For information on bulk purchases please contact Macmillan Corporate and Premium Sales Department at (800) 221-7945 x5442.

Distributed by Macmillan
First Printing

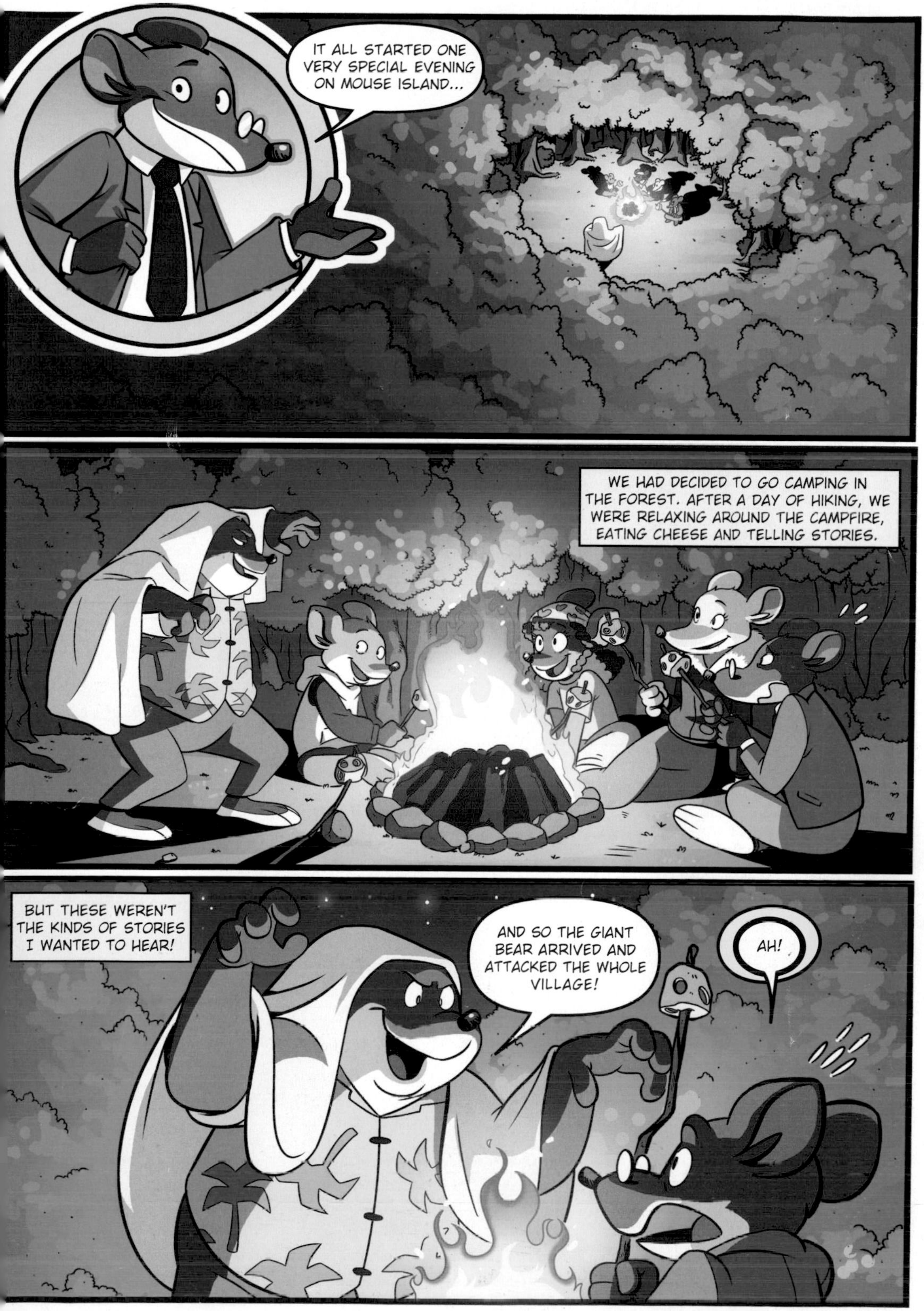

IT ALL STARTED ONE VERY SPECIAL EVENING ON MOUSE ISLAND...
WE HAD DECIDED TO GO CAMPING IN THE FOREST. AFTER A DAY OF HIKING, WE WERE RELAXING AROUND THE CAMPFIRE, EATING CHEESE AND TELLING STORIES.
BUT THESE WEREN'T THE KINDS OF STORIES I WANTED TO HEAR!
AND SO THE GIANT BEAR ARRIVED AND ATTACKED THE WHOLE VILLAGE!
AH!

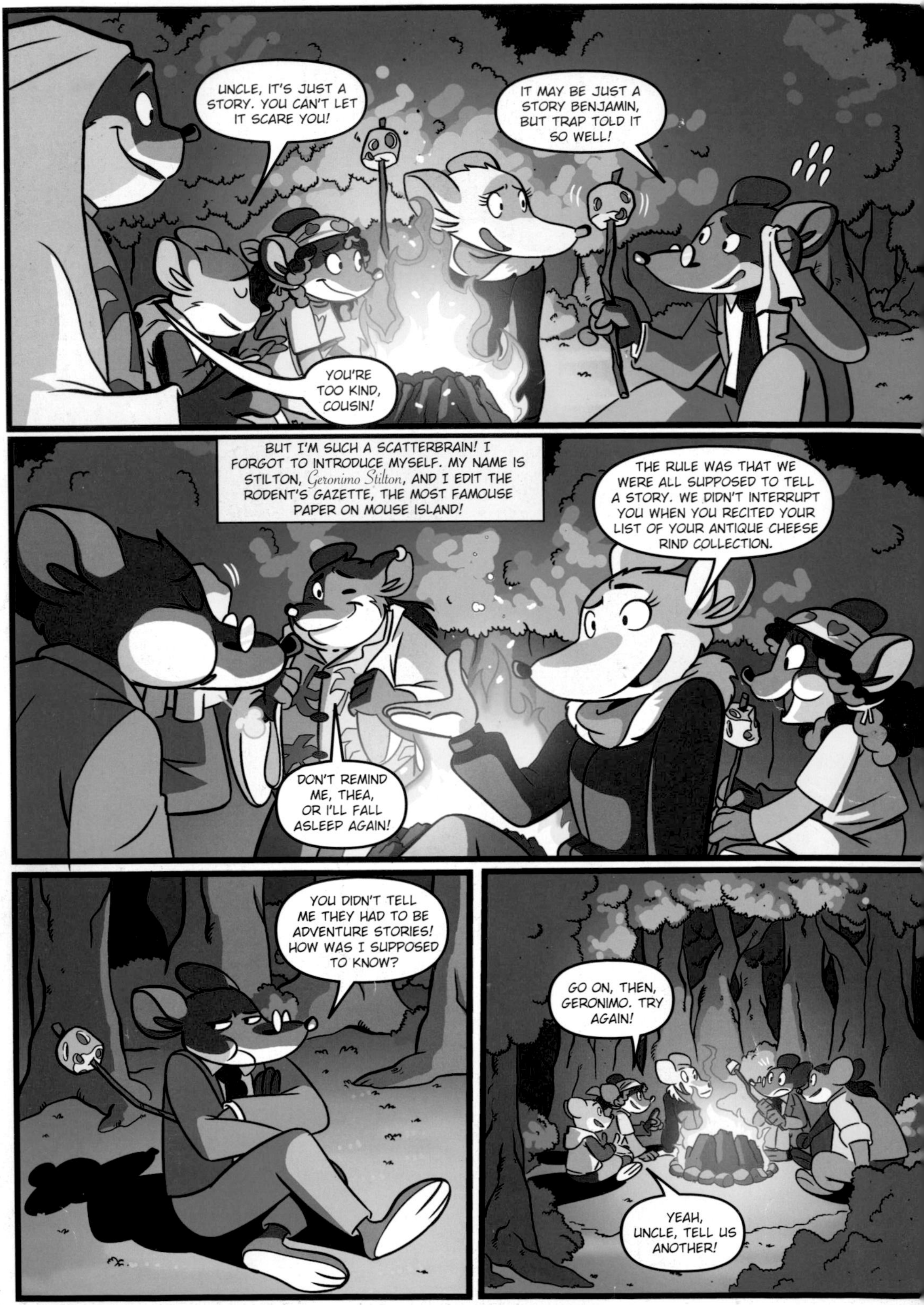

UNCLE, IT'S JUST A STORY. YOU CAN'T LET IT SCARE YOU!
IT MAY BE JUST A STORY BENJAMIN, BUT TRAP TOLD IT SO WELL!
YOU'RE TOO KIND, COUSIN!
BUT I'M SUCH A SCATTERBRAIN! I FORGOT TO INTRODUCE MYSELF. MY NAME IS STILTON, *Geronimo Stilton*, AND I EDIT THE RODENT'S GAZETTE, THE MOST FAMOUSE PAPER ON MOUSE ISLAND!
THE RULE WAS THAT WE WERE ALL SUPPOSED TO TELL A STORY. WE DIDN'T INTERRUPT YOU WHEN YOU RECITED YOUR LIST OF YOUR ANTIQUE CHEESE RIND COLLECTION.
DON'T REMIND ME, THEA, OR I'LL FALL ASLEEP AGAIN!
YOU DIDN'T TELL ME THEY HAD TO BE ADVENTURE STORIES! HOW WAS I SUPPOSED TO KNOW?
GO ON, THEN, GERONIMO. TRY AGAIN!
YEAH, UNCLE, TELL US ANOTHER!

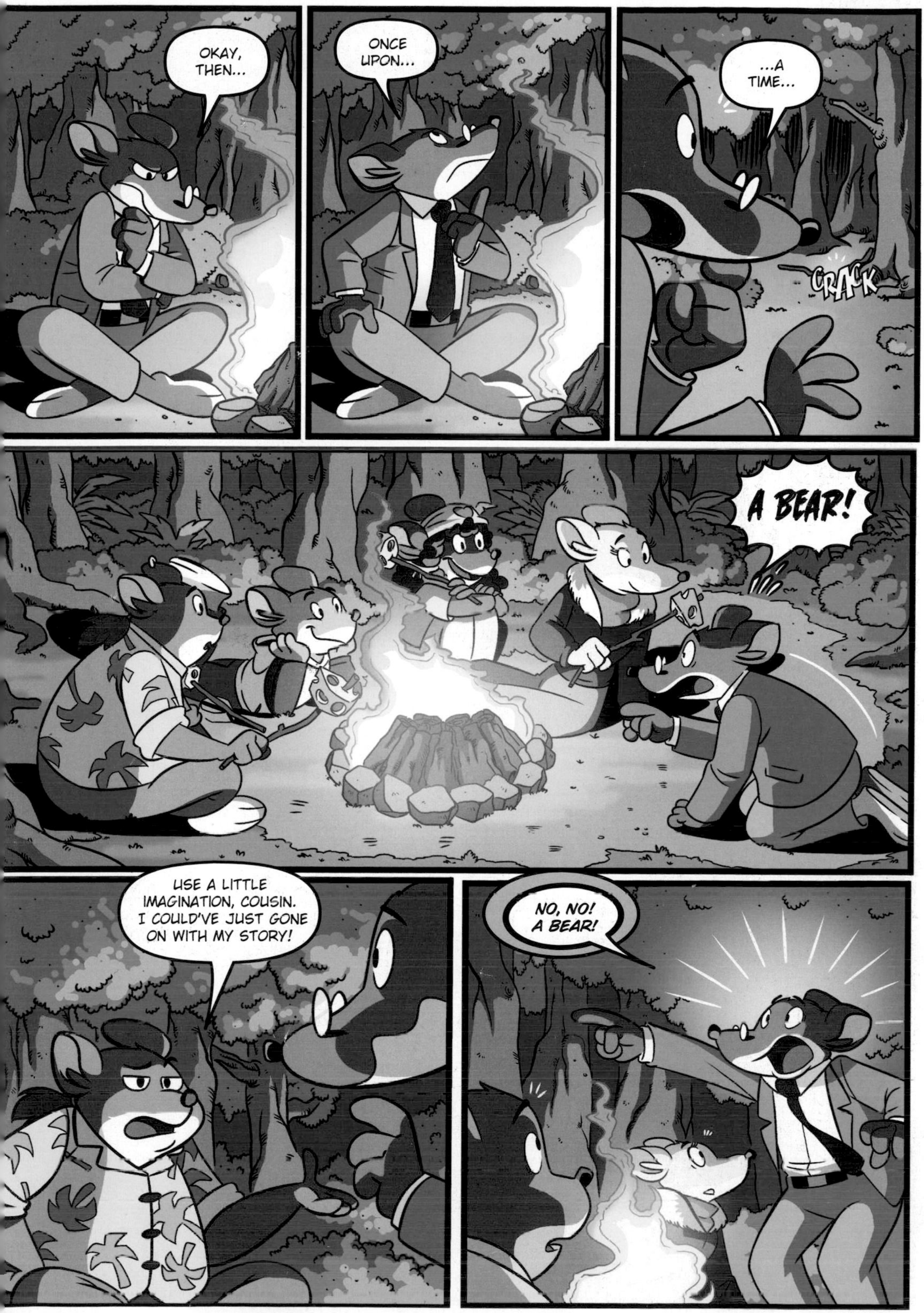

OKAY, THEN...
ONCE UPON...
...A TIME...
CRACK
A BEAR!
USE A LITTLE IMAGINATION, COUSIN. I COULD'VE JUST GONE ON WITH MY STORY!
NO, NO! A BEAR!

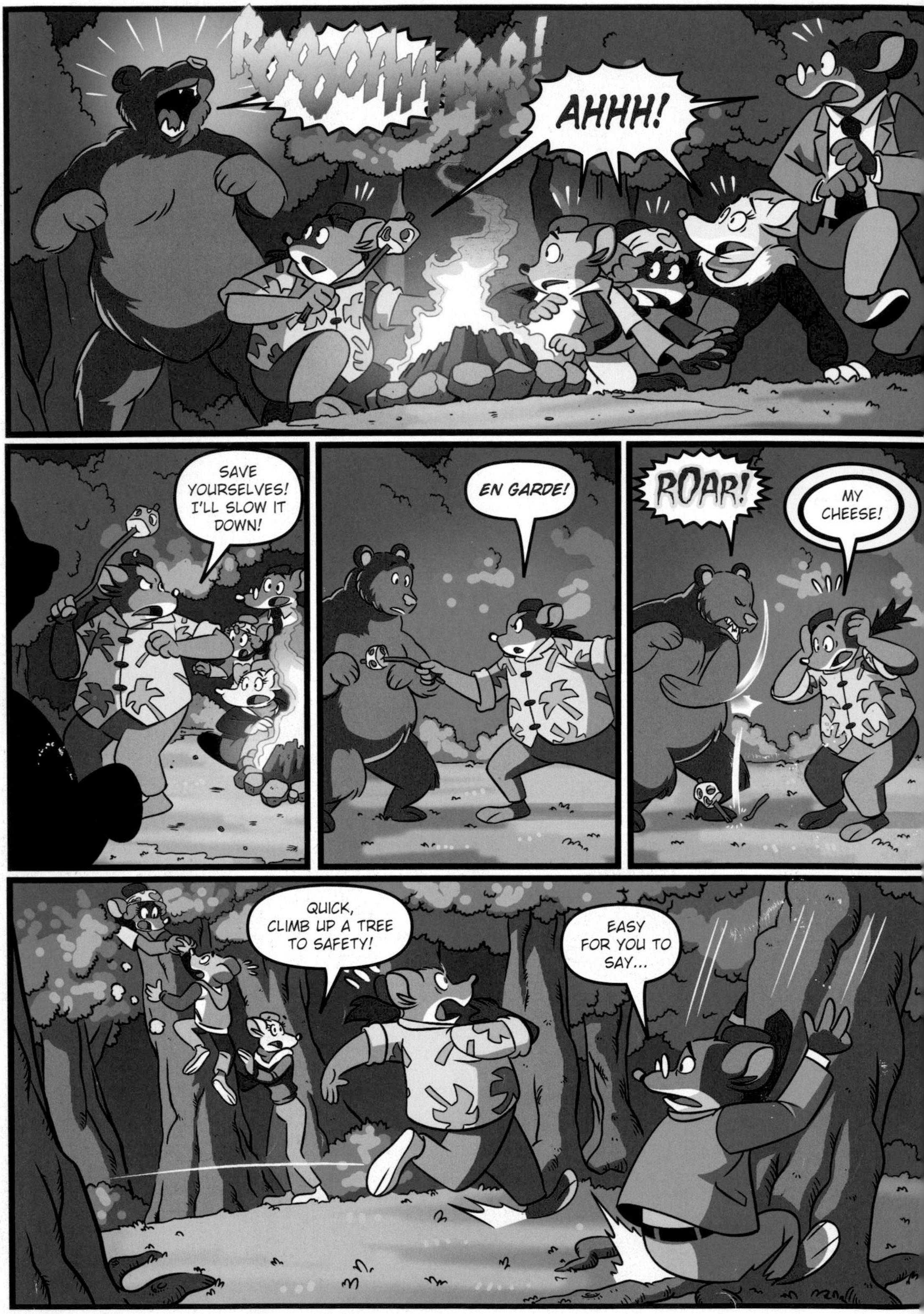
ROOOOAAARRR!
AHHH!
SAVE YOURSELVES! I'LL SLOW IT DOWN!
EN GARDE!
ROAR!
MY CHEESE!
QUICK, CLIMB UP A TREE TO SAFETY!
EASY FOR YOU TO SAY...

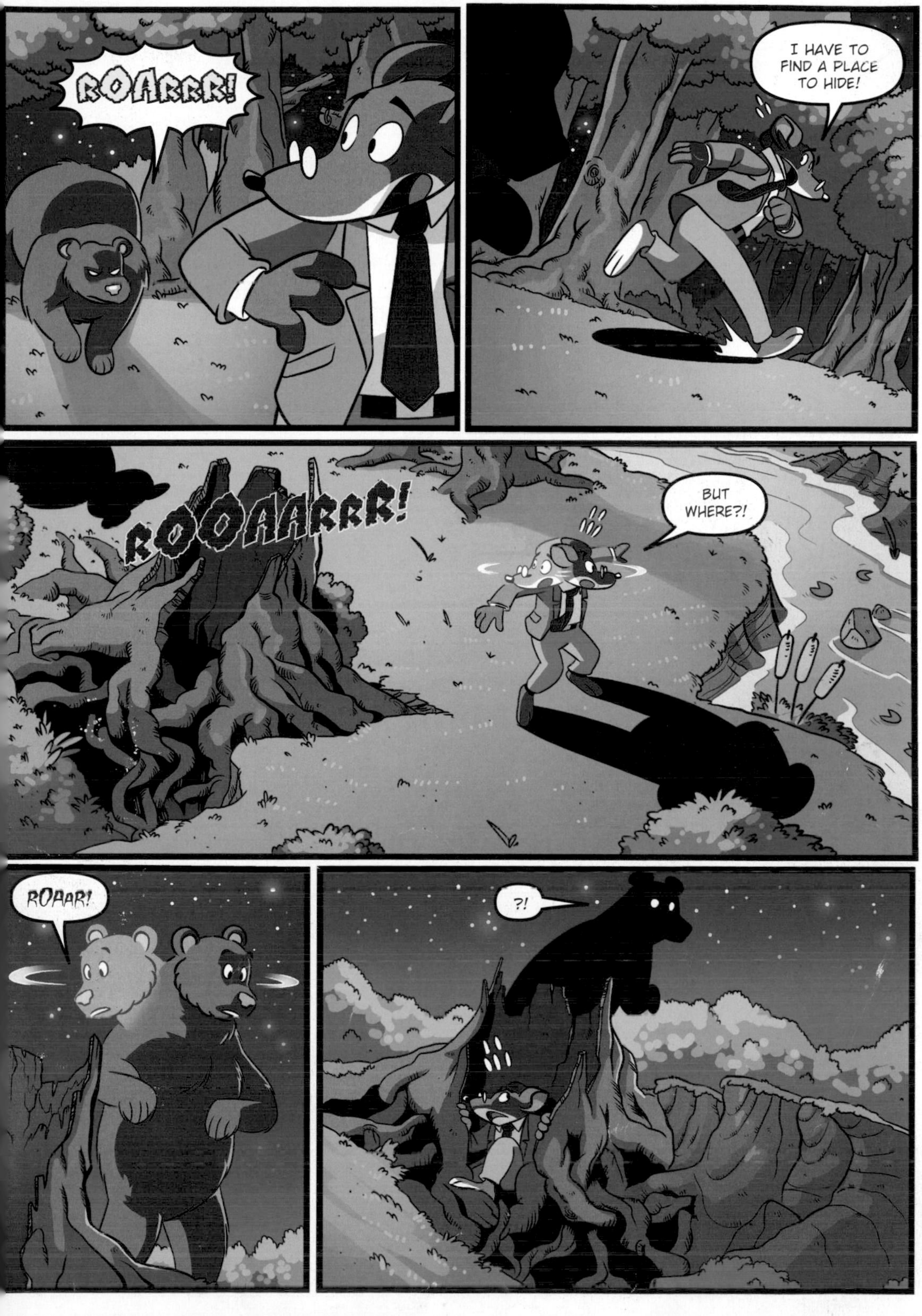

ROARRR!
I HAVE TO FIND A PLACE TO HIDE!
ROOOAARRRR!
BUT WHERE?!
ROAAR!
?!

-:HUFF:-...
-:PUFF:-...

ROAR?!

AHHH!

GERONIMO?

?!

OH MY WH-WH-ISKERS AND F-F-FUR...

YES, IT TALKS. IT TOOK ME A WHILE TO RESET THE VOICE CONTROLS IN THIS BEAR-DROID, BUT YOU DIDN'T HAVE TO KEEP RUNNING TO AND FRO!

THAT VOICE... IT'S PROFESSOR VON VOLT?!

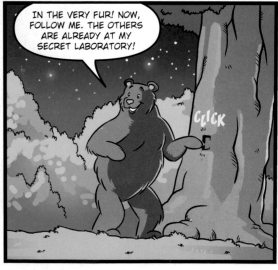

IN THE VERY FUR! NOW, FOLLOW ME. THE OTHERS ARE ALREADY AT MY SECRET LABORATORY!

CLICK

STEP INTO THIS CAPSULE. THE PNEUMATIC TRUNK WILL BRING YOU RIGHT HERE!

OKAY...

10

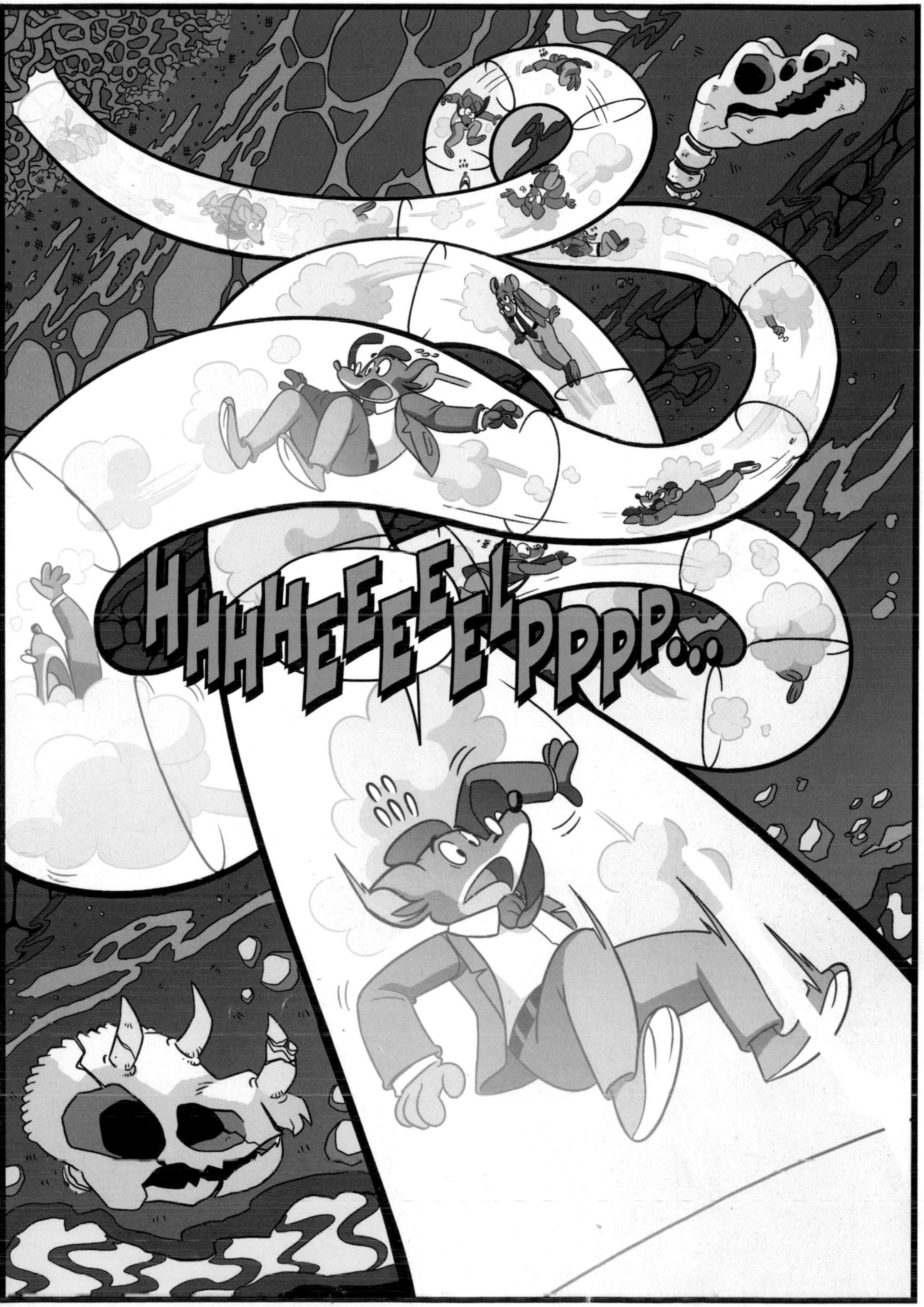
HHHHEEEEEELPPPP...

OOHHH! PROFESSOR, SOMEDAY I'M GOING TO GIVE YOU A PHONE TO CALL ME WITH!

GENIUS CAN'T BE EXPRESSED THROUGH SUCH CONVENTIONAL MEANS OF COMMUNICATION.

WANT TO HAVE SOME FUN?!

TRAP, WHAT ARE YOU DOING DRESSED LIKE THAT?!

YOU SAID TO DRESS LIKE A SAILOR...

YES. NOT LIKE A PIRATE!

BUT...I WANTED A PARROT AND A PATCH ON MY EYE! OOF. I'LL GO CHANGE...

WHY DO WE HAVE TO DRESS LIKE SAILORS?

MY TEMPOGRAPH IS SHOWING AN ANOMALY! THE PIRATE CATS HAVE GONE BACK IN TIME TO CHANGE IT AS THEY PLEASE!

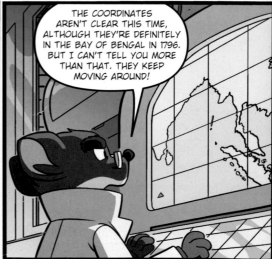

THE COORDINATES AREN'T CLEAR THIS TIME, ALTHOUGH THEY'RE DEFINITELY IN THE BAY OF BENGAL IN 1796. BUT I CAN'T TELL YOU MORE THAN THAT. THEY KEEP MOVING AROUND!

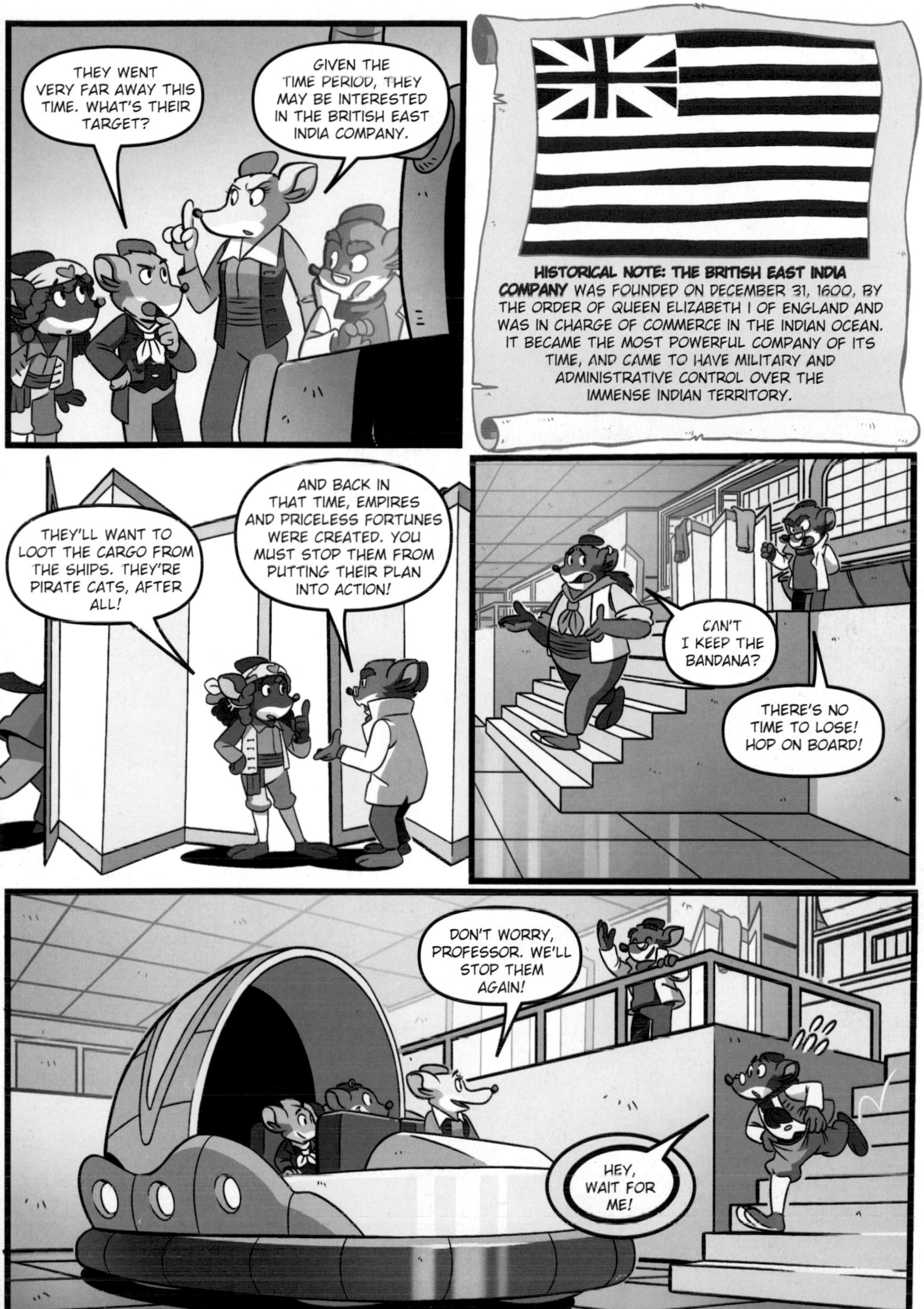
THEY WENT VERY FAR AWAY THIS TIME. WHAT'S THEIR TARGET?
GIVEN THE TIME PERIOD, THEY MAY BE INTERESTED IN THE BRITISH EAST INDIA COMPANY.
HISTORICAL NOTE: THE BRITISH EAST INDIA COMPANY WAS FOUNDED ON DECEMBER 31, 1600, BY THE ORDER OF QUEEN ELIZABETH I OF ENGLAND AND WAS IN CHARGE OF COMMERCE IN THE INDIAN OCEAN. IT BECAME THE MOST POWERFUL COMPANY OF ITS TIME, AND CAME TO HAVE MILITARY AND ADMINISTRATIVE CONTROL OVER THE IMMENSE INDIAN TERRITORY.
THEY'LL WANT TO LOOT THE CARGO FROM THE SHIPS. THEY'RE PIRATE CATS, AFTER ALL!
AND BACK IN THAT TIME, EMPIRES AND PRICELESS FORTUNES WERE CREATED. YOU MUST STOP THEM FROM PUTTING THEIR PLAN INTO ACTION!
CAN'T I KEEP THE BANDANA?
THERE'S NO TIME TO LOSE! HOP ON BOARD!
DON'T WORRY, PROFESSOR. WE'LL STOP THEM AGAIN!
HEY, WAIT FOR ME!

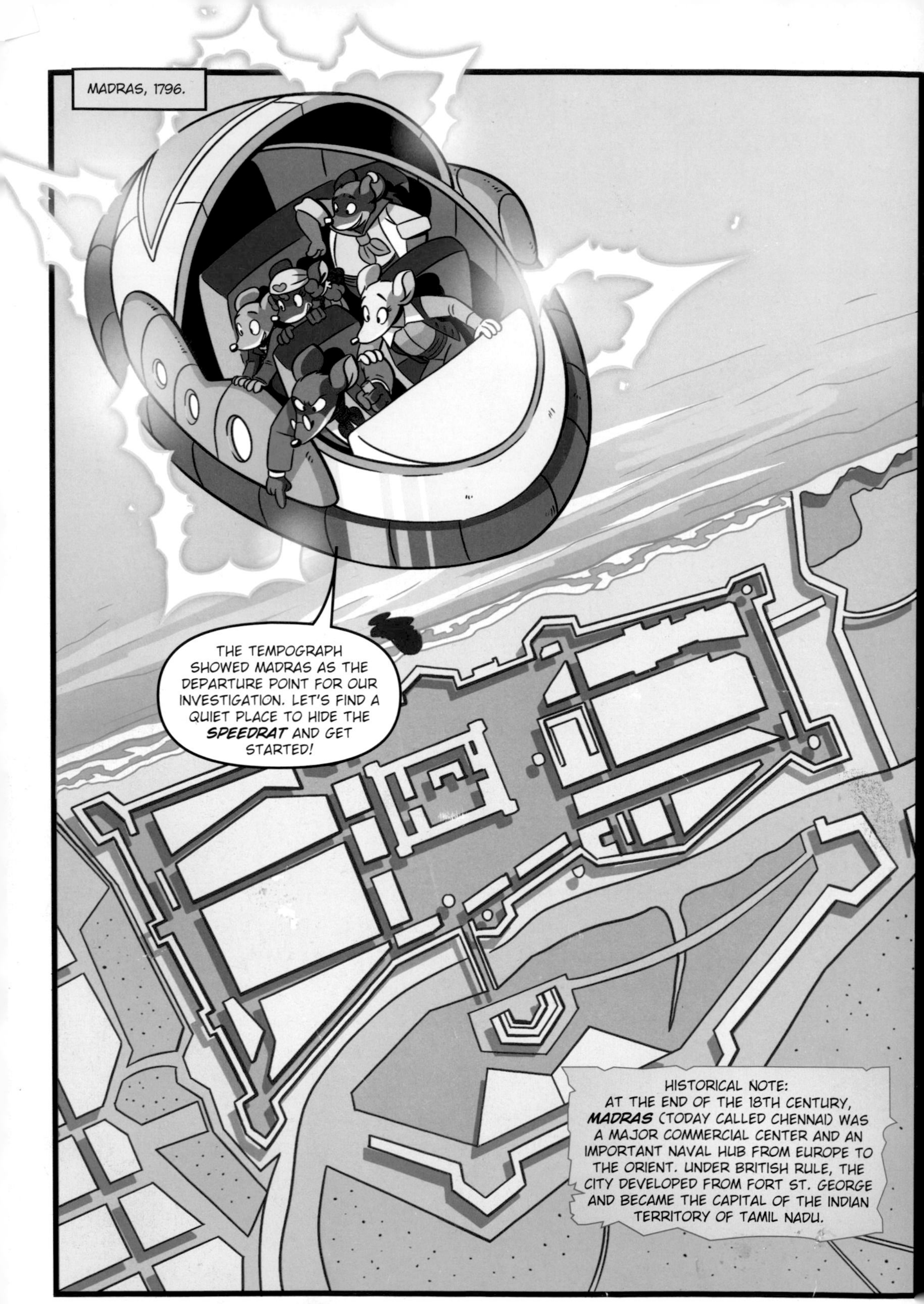
MADRAS, 1796.
THE TEMPOGRAPH SHOWED MADRAS AS THE DEPARTURE POINT FOR OUR INVESTIGATION. LET'S FIND A QUIET PLACE TO HIDE THE SPEEDRAT AND GET STARTED!
HISTORICAL NOTE: AT THE END OF THE 18TH CENTURY, MADRAS (TODAY CALLED CHENNAI) WAS A MAJOR COMMERCIAL CENTER AND AN IMPORTANT NAVAL HUB FROM EUROPE TO THE ORIENT. UNDER BRITISH RULE, THE CITY DEVELOPED FROM FORT ST. GEORGE AND BECAME THE CAPITAL OF THE INDIAN TERRITORY OF TAMIL NADU.

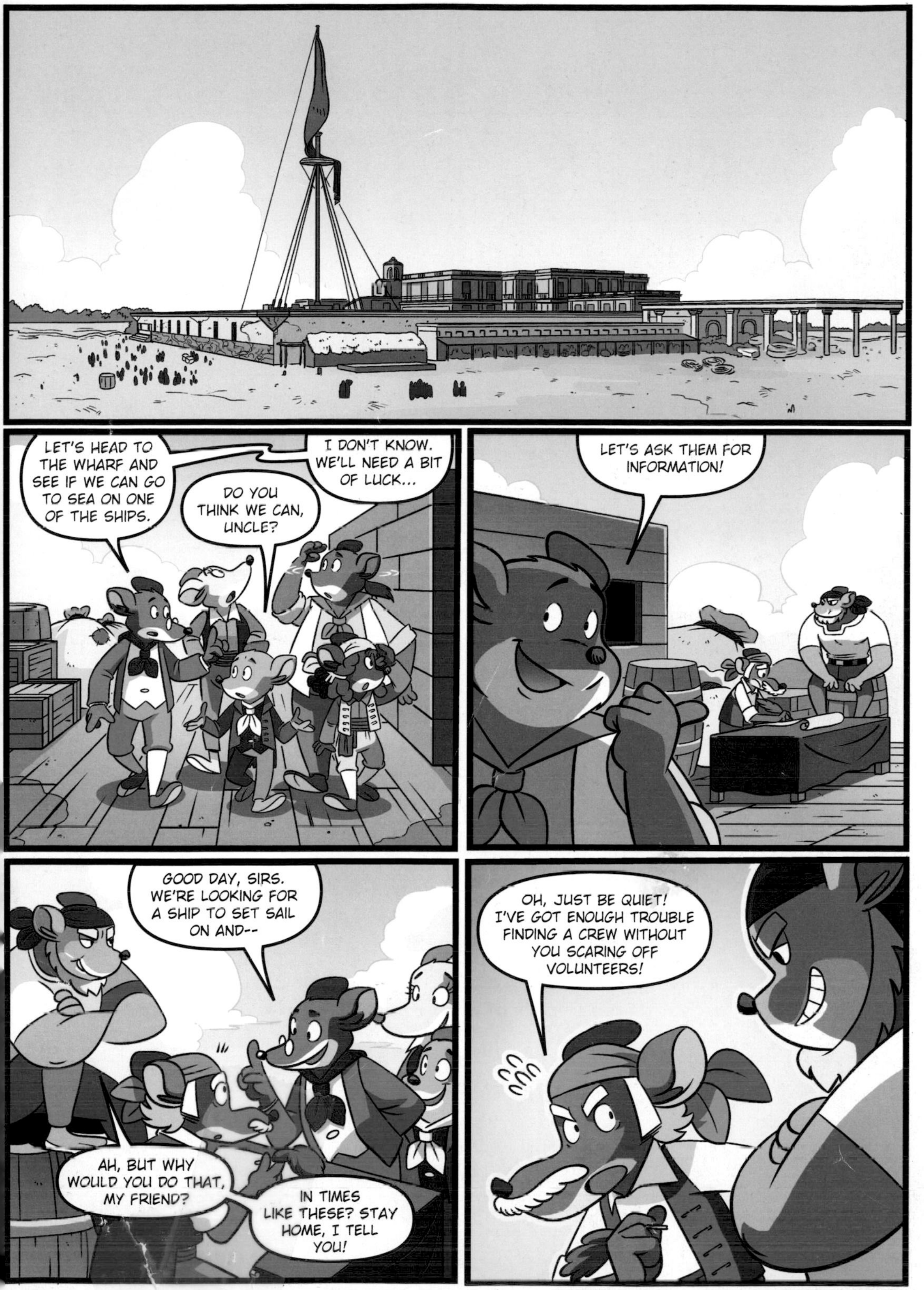
LET'S HEAD TO THE WHARF AND SEE IF WE CAN GO TO SEA ON ONE OF THE SHIPS.
DO YOU THINK WE CAN, UNCLE?
I DON'T KNOW. WE'LL NEED A BIT OF LUCK...
LET'S ASK THEM FOR INFORMATION!
GOOD DAY, SIRS. WE'RE LOOKING FOR A SHIP TO SET SAIL ON AND--
AH, BUT WHY WOULD YOU DO THAT, MY FRIEND?
IN TIMES LIKE THESE? STAY HOME, I TELL YOU!
OH, JUST BE QUIET! I'VE GOT ENOUGH TROUBLE FINDING A CREW WITHOUT YOU SCARING OFF VOLUNTEERS!

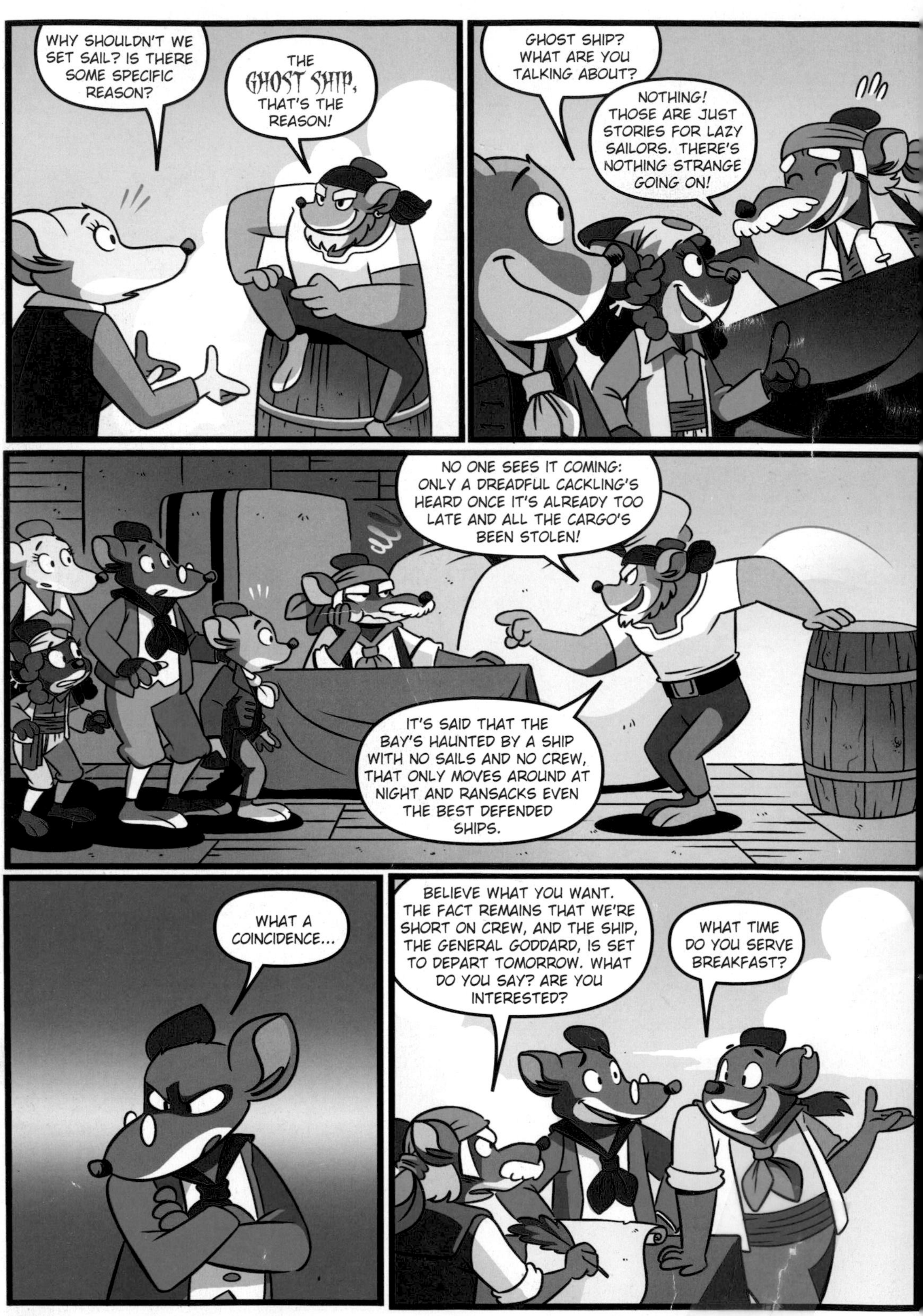

WHY SHOULDN'T WE SET SAIL? IS THERE SOME SPECIFIC REASON?
THE GHOST SHIP, THAT'S THE REASON!
GHOST SHIP? WHAT ARE YOU TALKING ABOUT?
NOTHING! THOSE ARE JUST STORIES FOR LAZY SAILORS. THERE'S NOTHING STRANGE GOING ON!
IT'S SAID THAT THE BAY'S HAUNTED BY A SHIP WITH NO SAILS AND NO CREW, THAT ONLY MOVES AROUND AT NIGHT AND RANSACKS EVEN THE BEST DEFENDED SHIPS.
NO ONE SEES IT COMING: ONLY A DREADFUL CACKLING'S HEARD ONCE IT'S ALREADY TOO LATE AND ALL THE CARGO'S BEEN STOLEN!
WHAT A COINCIDENCE...
BELIEVE WHAT YOU WANT. THE FACT REMAINS THAT WE'RE SHORT ON CREW, AND THE SHIP, THE GENERAL GODDARD, IS SET TO DEPART TOMORROW. WHAT DO YOU SAY? ARE YOU INTERESTED?
WHAT TIME DO YOU SERVE BREAKFAST?

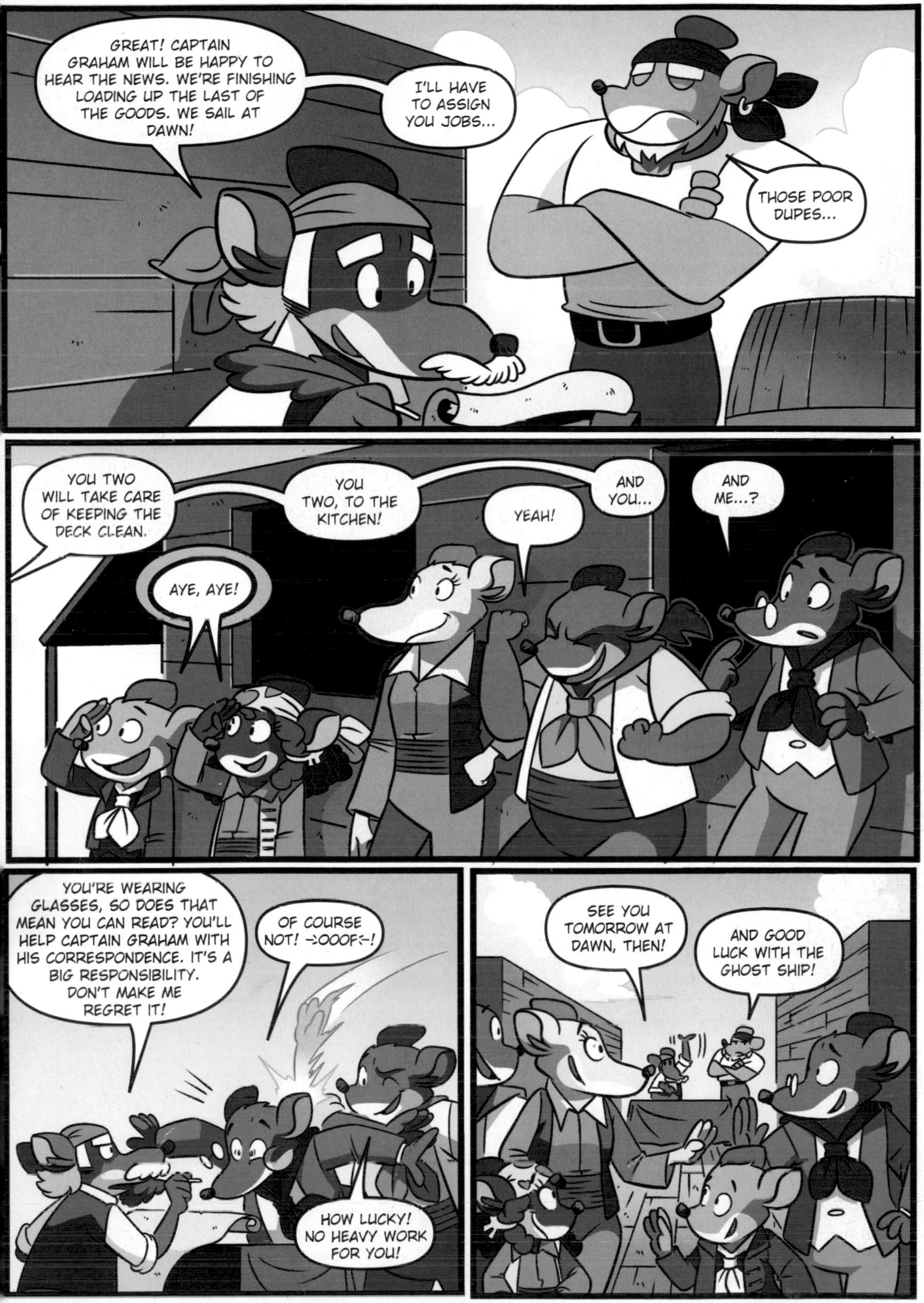
GREAT! CAPTAIN GRAHAM WILL BE HAPPY TO HEAR THE NEWS. WE'RE FINISHING LOADING UP THE LAST OF THE GOODS. WE SAIL AT DAWN!
I'LL HAVE TO ASSIGN YOU JOBS...
THOSE POOR DUPES...
YOU TWO WILL TAKE CARE OF KEEPING THE DECK CLEAN.
AYE, AYE!
YOU TWO, TO THE KITCHEN!
YEAH!
AND YOU...
AND ME...?
YOU'RE WEARING GLASSES, SO DOES THAT MEAN YOU CAN READ? YOU'LL HELP CAPTAIN GRAHAM WITH HIS CORRESPONDENCE. IT'S A BIG RESPONSIBILITY. DON'T MAKE ME REGRET IT!
OF COURSE NOT! ->OOOF<-!
HOW LUCKY! NO HEAVY WORK FOR YOU!
SEE YOU TOMORROW AT DAWN, THEN!
AND GOOD LUCK WITH THE GHOST SHIP!

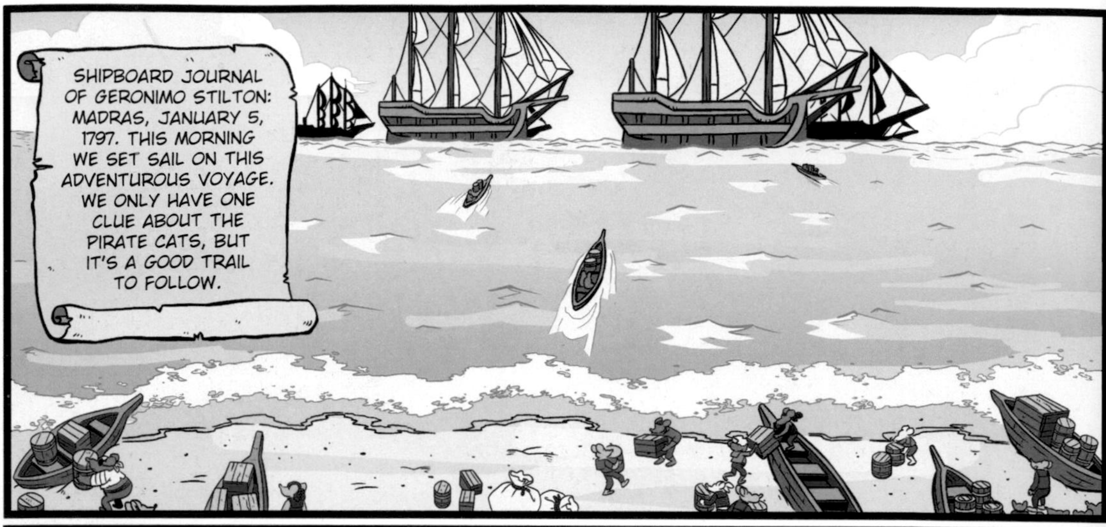
SHIPBOARD JOURNAL OF GERONIMO STILTON: MADRAS, JANUARY 5, 1797. THIS MORNING WE SET SAIL ON THIS ADVENTUROUS VOYAGE. WE ONLY HAVE ONE CLUE ABOUT THE PIRATE CATS, BUT IT'S A GOOD TRAIL TO FOLLOW.

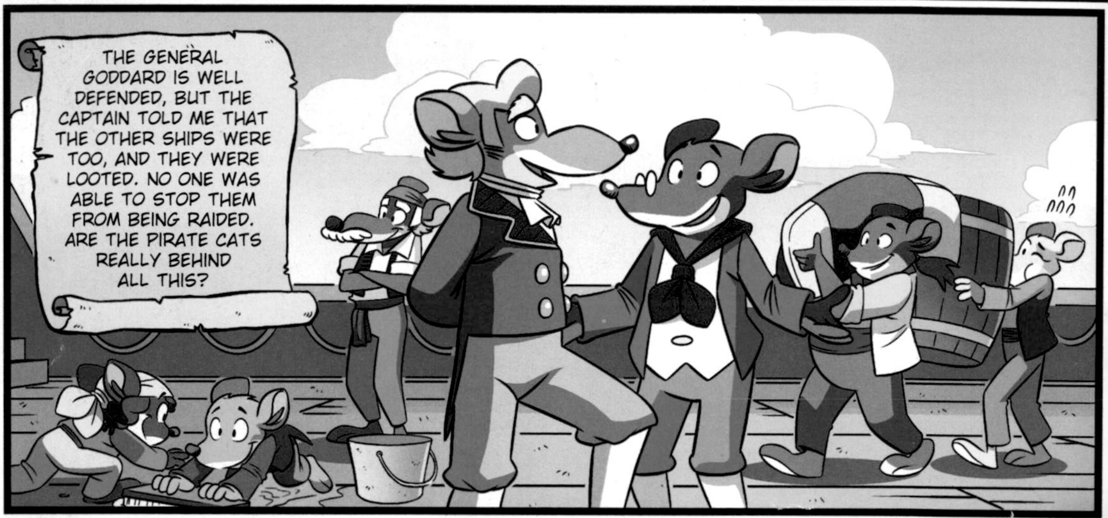
THE GENERAL GODDARD IS WELL DEFENDED, BUT THE CAPTAIN TOLD ME THAT THE OTHER SHIPS WERE TOO, AND THEY WERE LOOTED. NO ONE WAS ABLE TO STOP THEM FROM BEING RAIDED. ARE THE PIRATE CATS REALLY BEHIND ALL THIS?

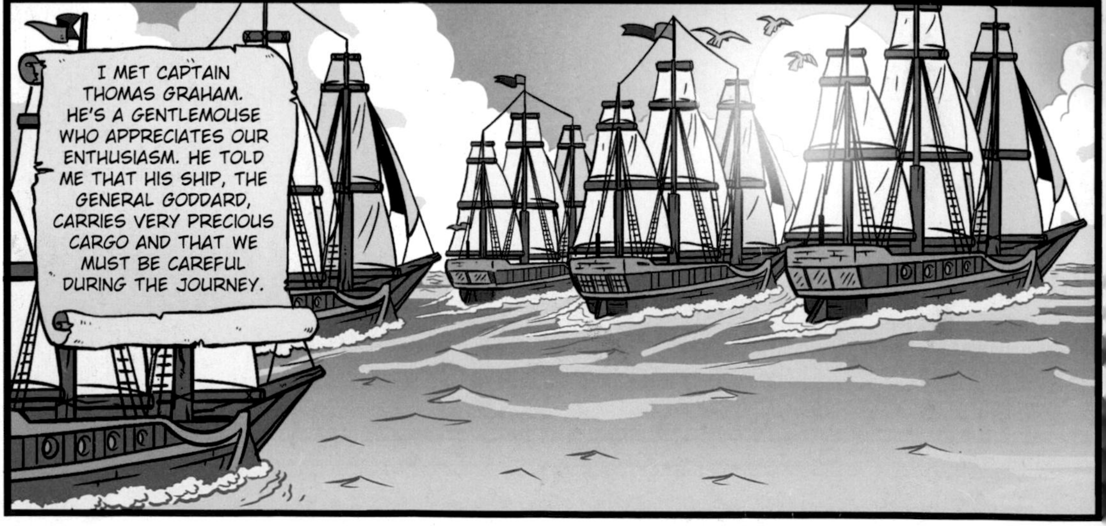
I MET CAPTAIN THOMAS GRAHAM. HE'S A GENTLEMOUSE WHO APPRECIATES OUR ENTHUSIASM. HE TOLD ME THAT HIS SHIP, THE GENERAL GODDARD, CARRIES VERY PRECIOUS CARGO AND THAT WE MUST BE CAREFUL DURING THE JOURNEY.

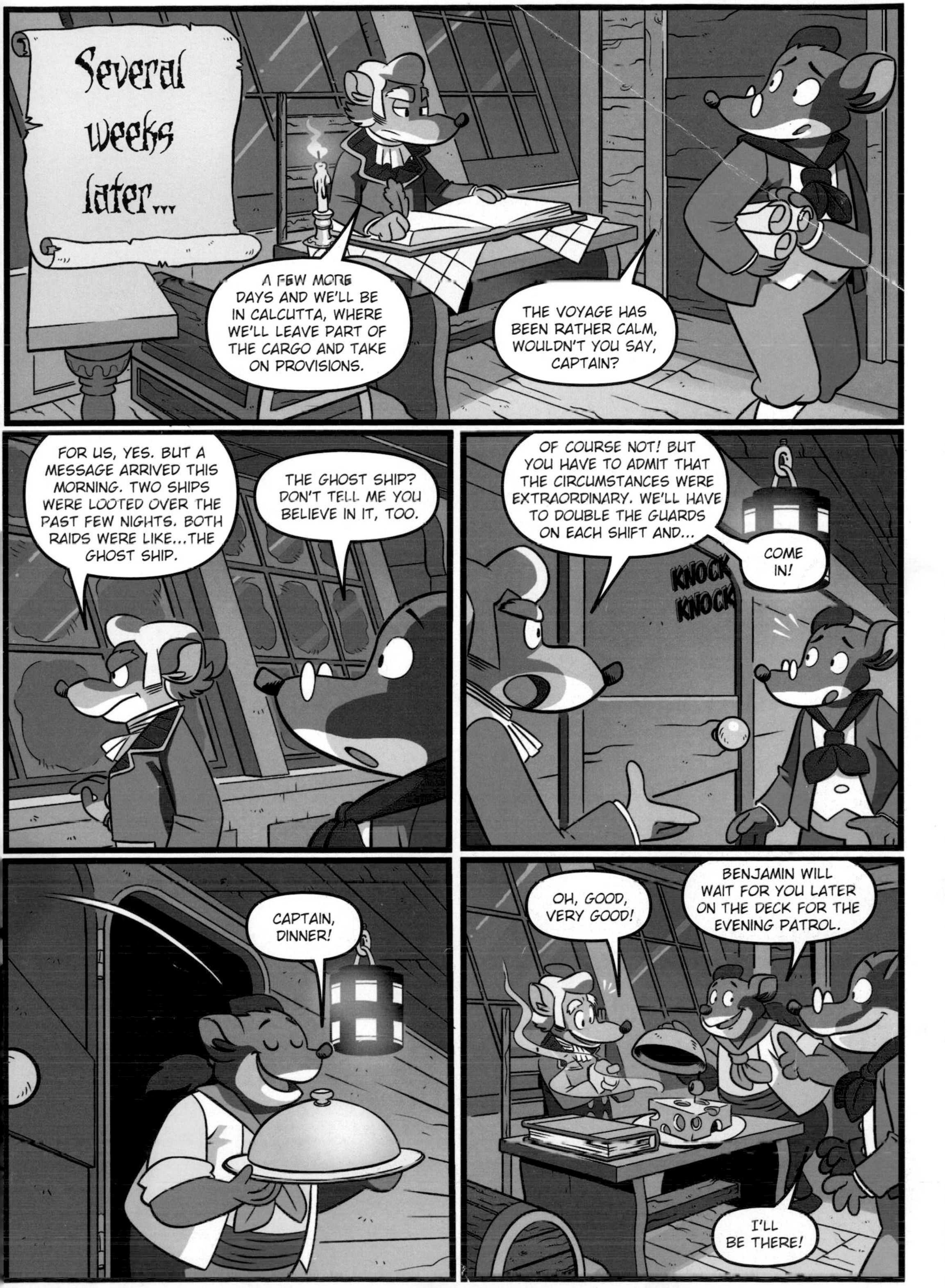
Several weeks later...
A FEW MORE DAYS AND WE'LL BE IN CALCUTTA, WHERE WE'LL LEAVE PART OF THE CARGO AND TAKE ON PROVISIONS.
THE VOYAGE HAS BEEN RATHER CALM, WOULDN'T YOU SAY, CAPTAIN?
FOR US, YES. BUT A MESSAGE ARRIVED THIS MORNING. TWO SHIPS WERE LOOTED OVER THE PAST FEW NIGHTS. BOTH RAIDS WERE LIKE...THE GHOST SHIP.
THE GHOST SHIP? DON'T TELL ME YOU BELIEVE IN IT, TOO.
OF COURSE NOT! BUT YOU HAVE TO ADMIT THAT THE CIRCUMSTANCES WERE EXTRAORDINARY. WE'LL HAVE TO DOUBLE THE GUARDS ON EACH SHIFT AND...
KNOCK KNOCK
COME IN!
CAPTAIN, DINNER!
OH, GOOD, VERY GOOD!
BENJAMIN WILL WAIT FOR YOU LATER ON THE DECK FOR THE EVENING PATROL.
I'LL BE THERE!

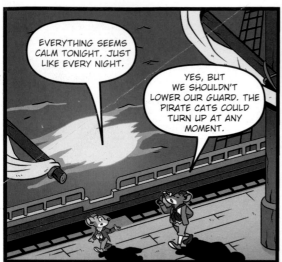

EVERYTHING SEEMS CALM TONIGHT. JUST LIKE EVERY NIGHT.

YES, BUT WE SHOULDN'T LOWER OUR GUARD. THE PIRATE CATS COULD TURN UP AT ANY MOMENT.

WHAT IF IT'S NOT THEM? THAT IS...WHAT IF IT'S SOMETHING ELSE?

THEY'RE PIRATES—IT'S IN THEIR NATURE TO PIRATE. BUT I CAN'T FIGURE OUT WHY THEY'RE RETURNING TO THE PAST TO BE PIRATES. WHAT CAN THEY POSSIBLY GAIN HERE?

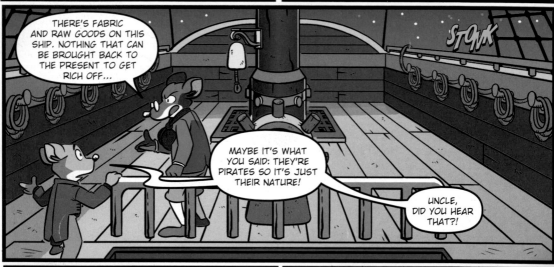

THERE'S FABRIC AND RAW GOODS ON THIS SHIP. NOTHING THAT CAN BE BROUGHT BACK TO THE PRESENT TO GET RICH OFF...

STONK

MAYBE IT'S WHAT YOU SAID: THEY'RE PIRATES SO IT'S JUST THEIR NATURE!

UNCLE, DID YOU HEAR THAT?!

IT CAME FROM OVER THERE!

CAN YOU SEE ANYTHING?

20

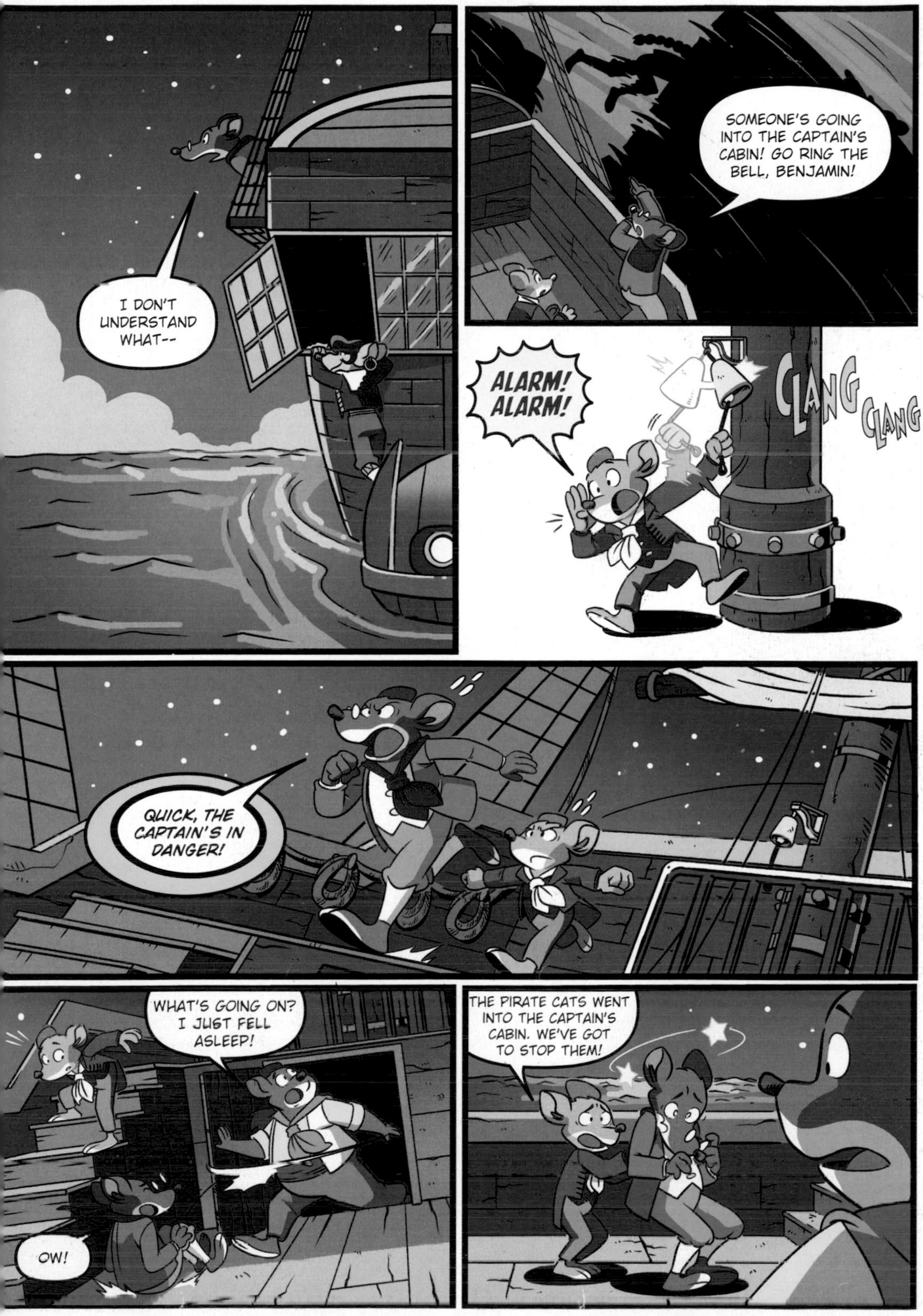
I DON'T UNDERSTAND WHAT--
SOMEONE'S GOING INTO THE CAPTAIN'S CABIN! GO RING THE BELL, BENJAMIN!
ALARM! ALARM!
CLANG CLANG
QUICK, THE CAPTAIN'S IN DANGER!
WHAT'S GOING ON? I JUST FELL ASLEEP!
OW!
THE PIRATE CATS WENT INTO THE CAPTAIN'S CABIN. WE'VE GOT TO STOP THEM!

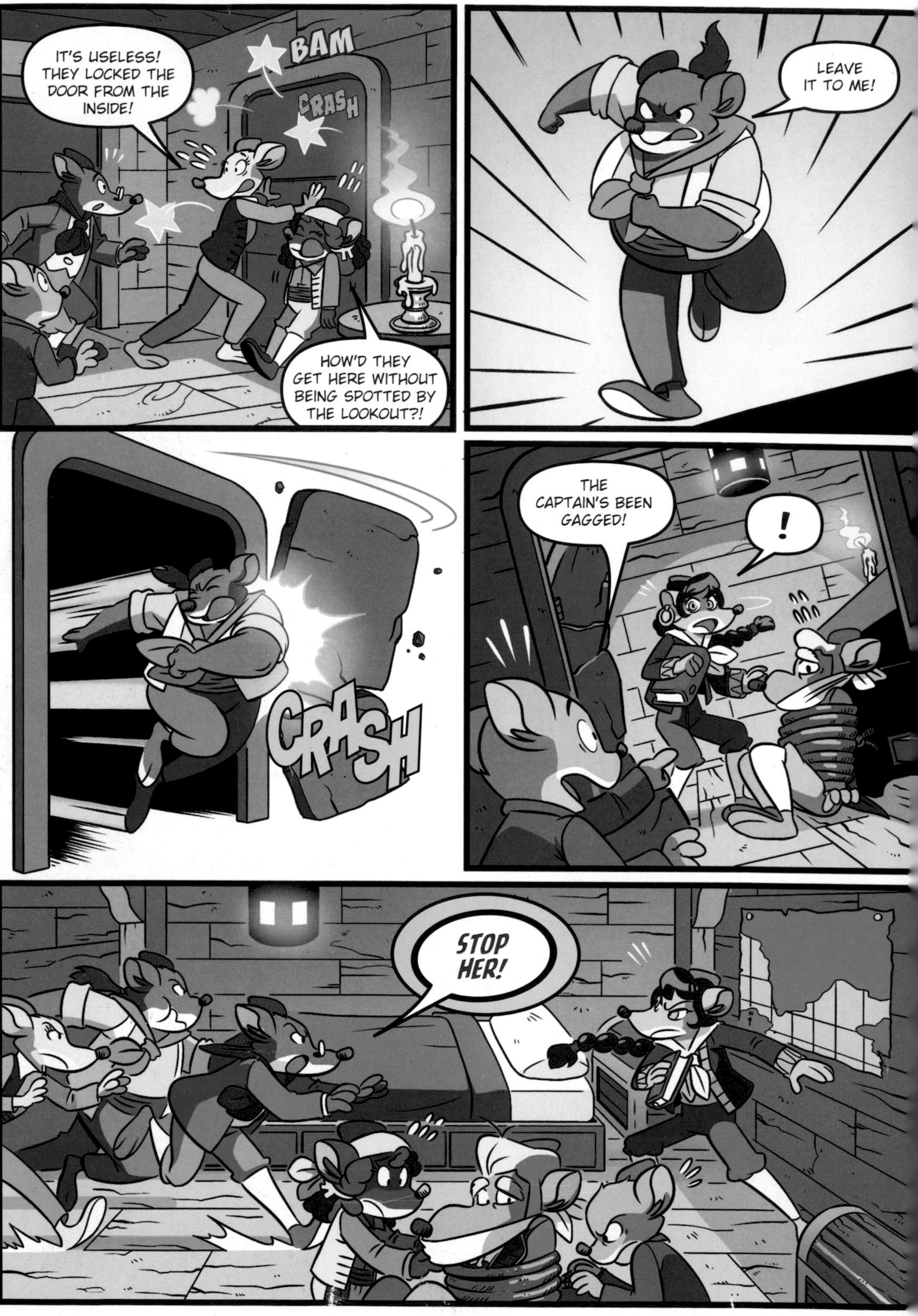
IT'S USELESS! THEY LOCKED THE DOOR FROM THE INSIDE!
BAM
CRASH
HOW'D THEY GET HERE WITHOUT BEING SPOTTED BY THE LOOKOUT?!
LEAVE IT TO ME!
CRASH
THE CAPTAIN'S BEEN GAGGED!
!
STOP HER!

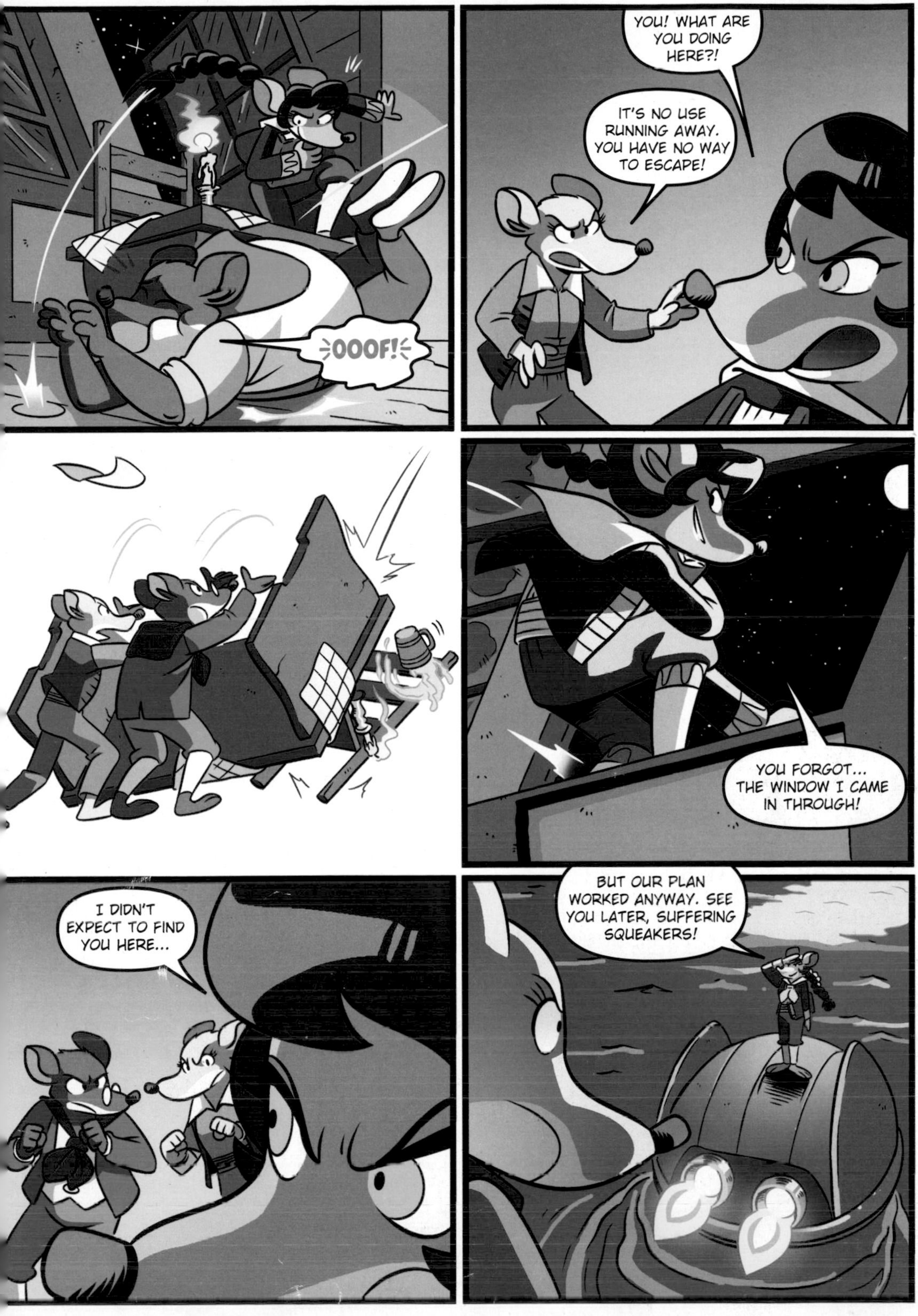
OOOF!
YOU! WHAT ARE YOU DOING HERE?!
IT'S NO USE RUNNING AWAY. YOU HAVE NO WAY TO ESCAPE!
YOU FORGOT... THE WINDOW I CAME IN THROUGH!
I DIDN'T EXPECT TO FIND YOU HERE...
BUT OUR PLAN WORKED ANYWAY. SEE YOU LATER, SUFFERING SQUEAKERS!

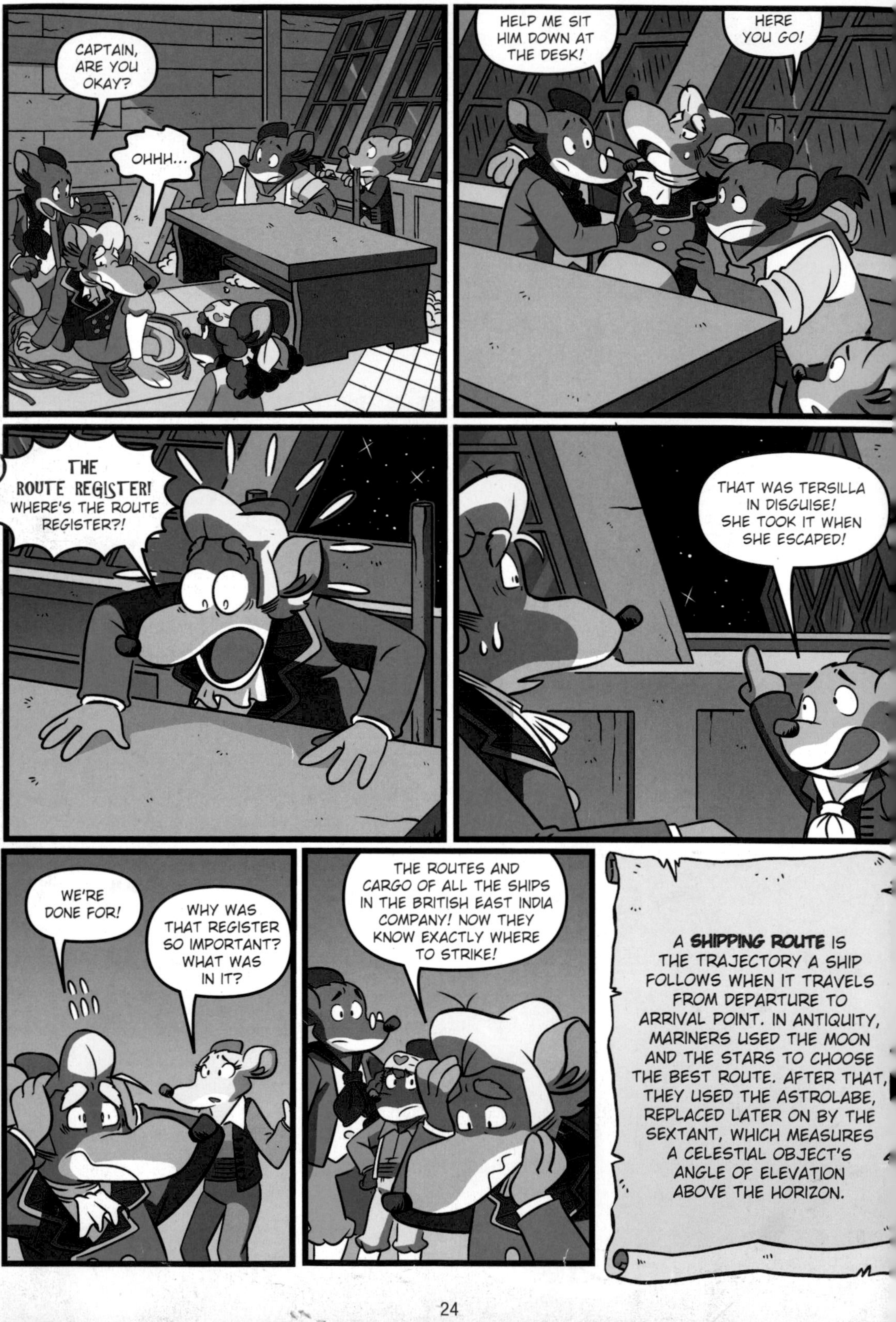
CAPTAIN, ARE YOU OKAY?
OHHH...
HELP ME SIT HIM DOWN AT THE DESK!
HERE YOU GO!
THE ROUTE REGISTER! WHERE'S THE ROUTE REGISTER?!
THAT WAS TERSILLA IN DISGUISE! SHE TOOK IT WHEN SHE ESCAPED!
WE'RE DONE FOR!
WHY WAS THAT REGISTER SO IMPORTANT? WHAT WAS IN IT?
THE ROUTES AND CARGO OF ALL THE SHIPS IN THE BRITISH EAST INDIA COMPANY! NOW THEY KNOW EXACTLY WHERE TO STRIKE!
A SHIPPING ROUTE IS THE TRAJECTORY A SHIP FOLLOWS WHEN IT TRAVELS FROM DEPARTURE TO ARRIVAL POINT. IN ANTIQUITY, MARINERS USED THE MOON AND THE STARS TO CHOOSE THE BEST ROUTE. AFTER THAT, THEY USED THE ASTROLABE, REPLACED LATER ON BY THE SEXTANT, WHICH MEASURES A CELESTIAL OBJECT'S ANGLE OF ELEVATION ABOVE THE HORIZON.

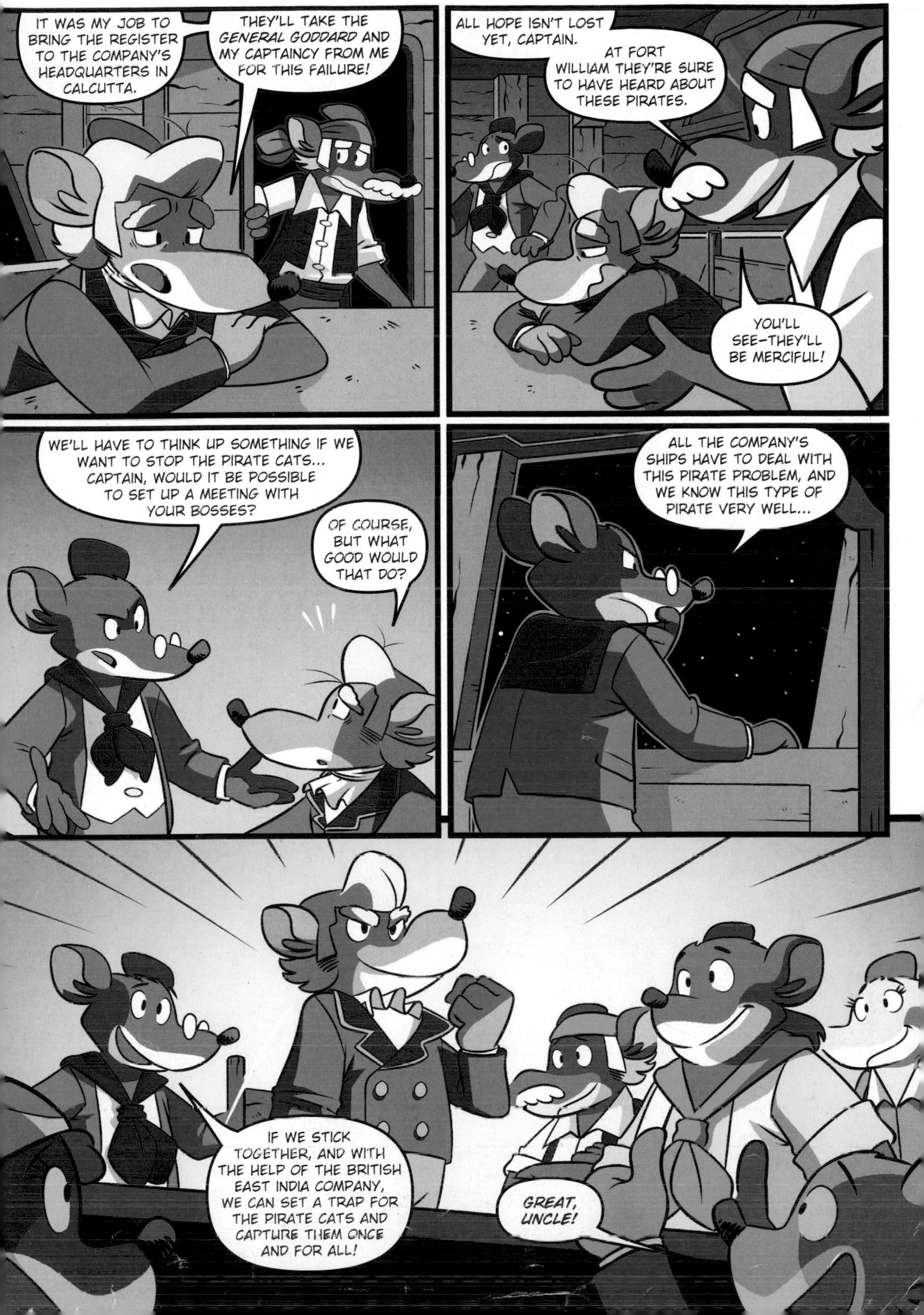
IT WAS MY JOB TO BRING THE REGISTER TO THE COMPANY'S HEADQUARTERS IN CALCUTTA.
THEY'LL TAKE THE *GENERAL GODDARD* AND MY CAPTAINCY FROM ME FOR THIS FAILURE!
ALL HOPE ISN'T LOST YET, CAPTAIN.
AT FORT WILLIAM THEY'RE SURE TO HAVE HEARD ABOUT THESE PIRATES.
YOU'LL SEE—THEY'LL BE MERCIFUL!
WE'LL HAVE TO THINK UP SOMETHING IF WE WANT TO STOP THE PIRATE CATS... CAPTAIN, WOULD IT BE POSSIBLE TO SET UP A MEETING WITH YOUR BOSSES?
OF COURSE, BUT WHAT GOOD WOULD THAT DO?
ALL THE COMPANY'S SHIPS HAVE TO DEAL WITH THIS PIRATE PROBLEM, AND WE KNOW THIS TYPE OF PIRATE VERY WELL...
IF WE STICK TOGETHER, AND WITH THE HELP OF THE BRITISH EAST INDIA COMPANY, WE CAN SET A TRAP FOR THE PIRATE CATS AND CAPTURE THEM ONCE AND FOR ALL!
GREAT, UNCLE!

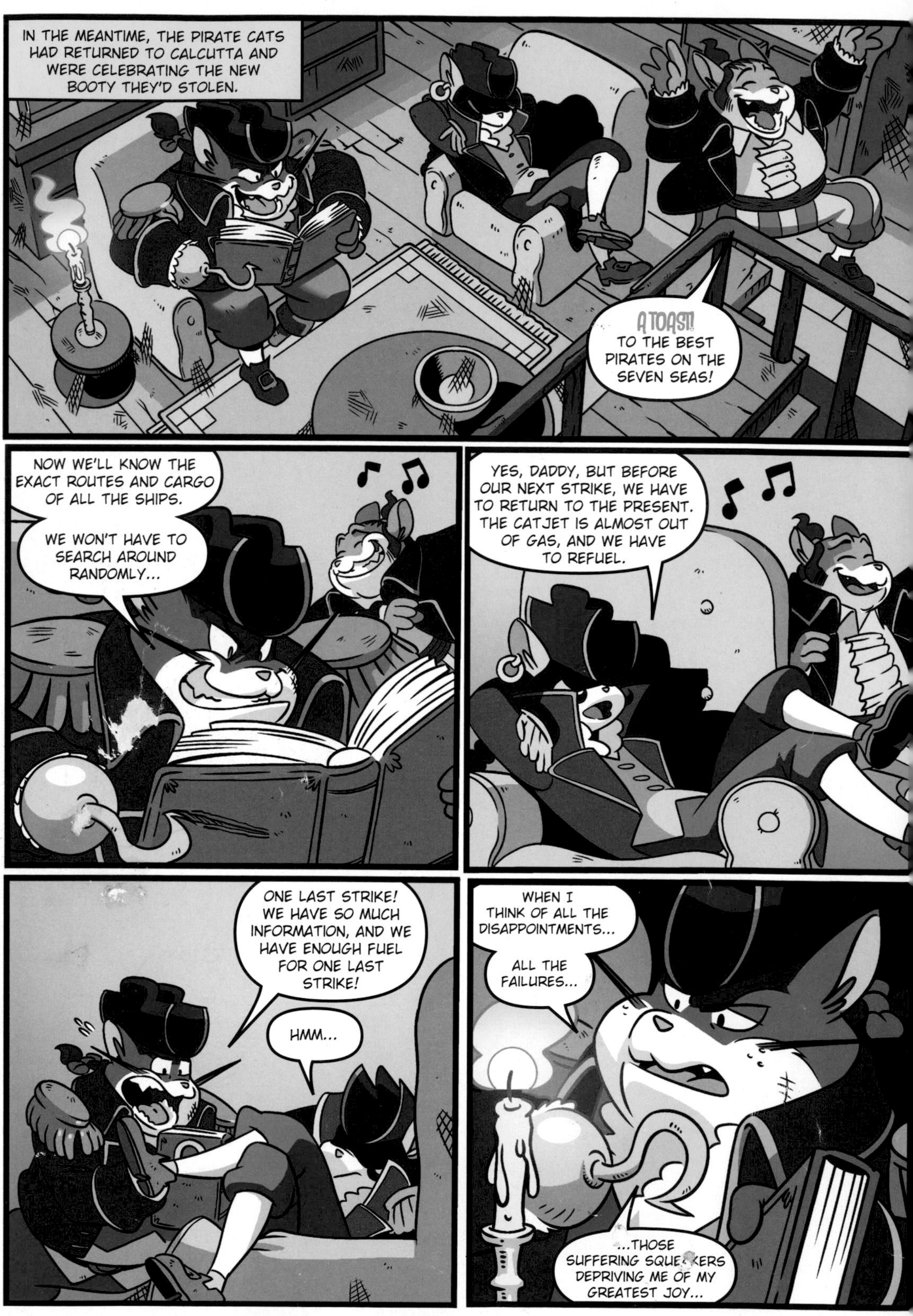
IN THE MEANTIME, THE PIRATE CATS HAD RETURNED TO CALCUTTA AND WERE CELEBRATING THE NEW BOOTY THEY'D STOLEN.
A TOAST! TO THE BEST PIRATES ON THE SEVEN SEAS!
NOW WE'LL KNOW THE EXACT ROUTES AND CARGO OF ALL THE SHIPS.
WE WON'T HAVE TO SEARCH AROUND RANDOMLY...
YES, DADDY, BUT BEFORE OUR NEXT STRIKE, WE HAVE TO RETURN TO THE PRESENT. THE CATJET IS ALMOST OUT OF GAS, AND WE HAVE TO REFUEL.
ONE LAST STRIKE! WE HAVE SO MUCH INFORMATION, AND WE HAVE ENOUGH FUEL FOR ONE LAST STRIKE!
HMM...
WHEN I THINK OF ALL THE DISAPPOINTMENTS...
ALL THE FAILURES...
...THOSE SUFFERING SQUEAKERS DEPRIVING ME OF MY GREATEST JOY...

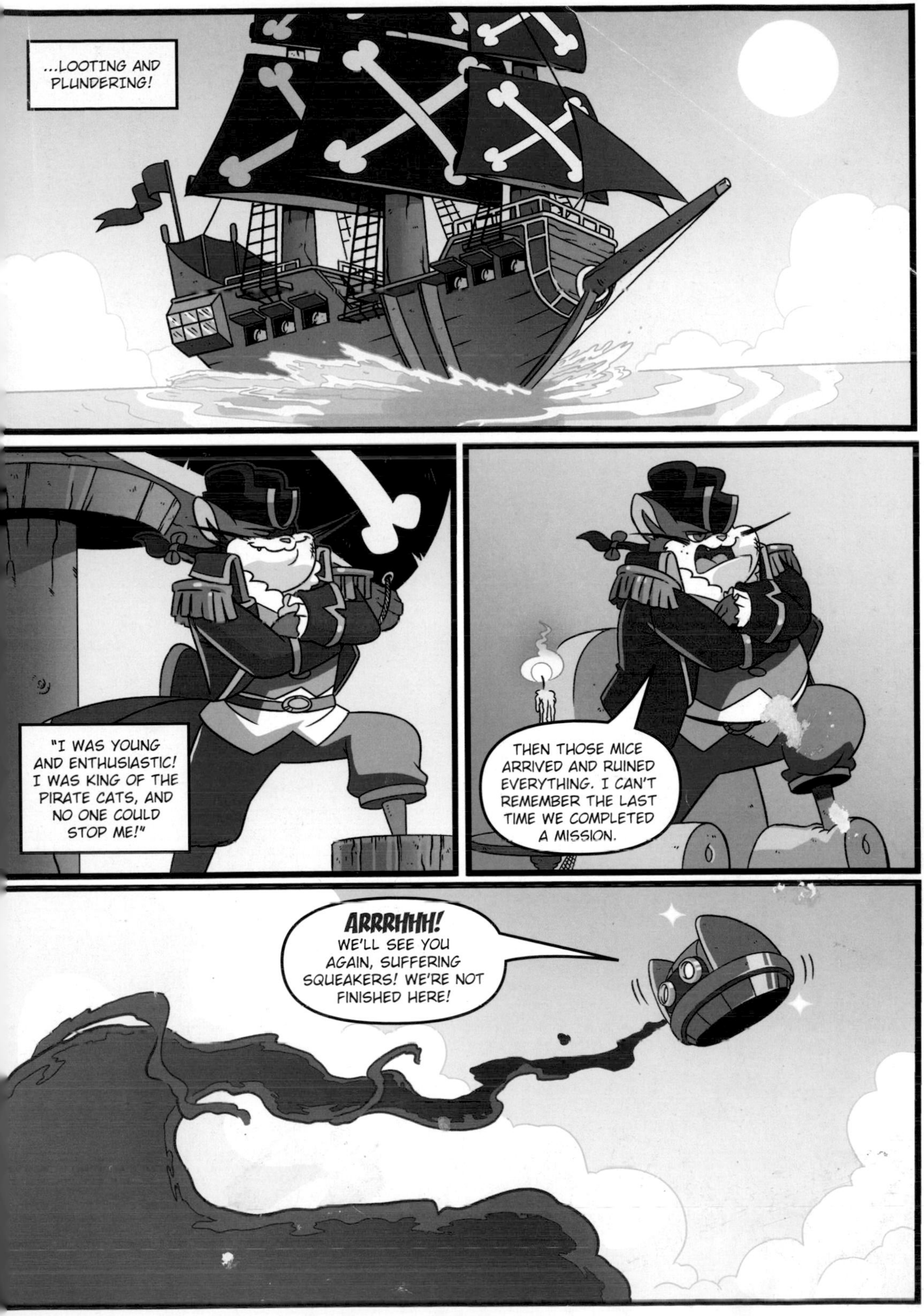
...LOOTING AND PLUNDERING!
"I WAS YOUNG AND ENTHUSIASTIC! I WAS KING OF THE PIRATE CATS, AND NO ONE COULD STOP ME!"
THEN THOSE MICE ARRIVED AND RUINED EVERYTHING. I CAN'T REMEMBER THE LAST TIME WE COMPLETED A MISSION.
ARRRHHH! WE'LL SEE YOU AGAIN, SUFFERING SQUEAKERS! WE'RE NOT FINISHED HERE!

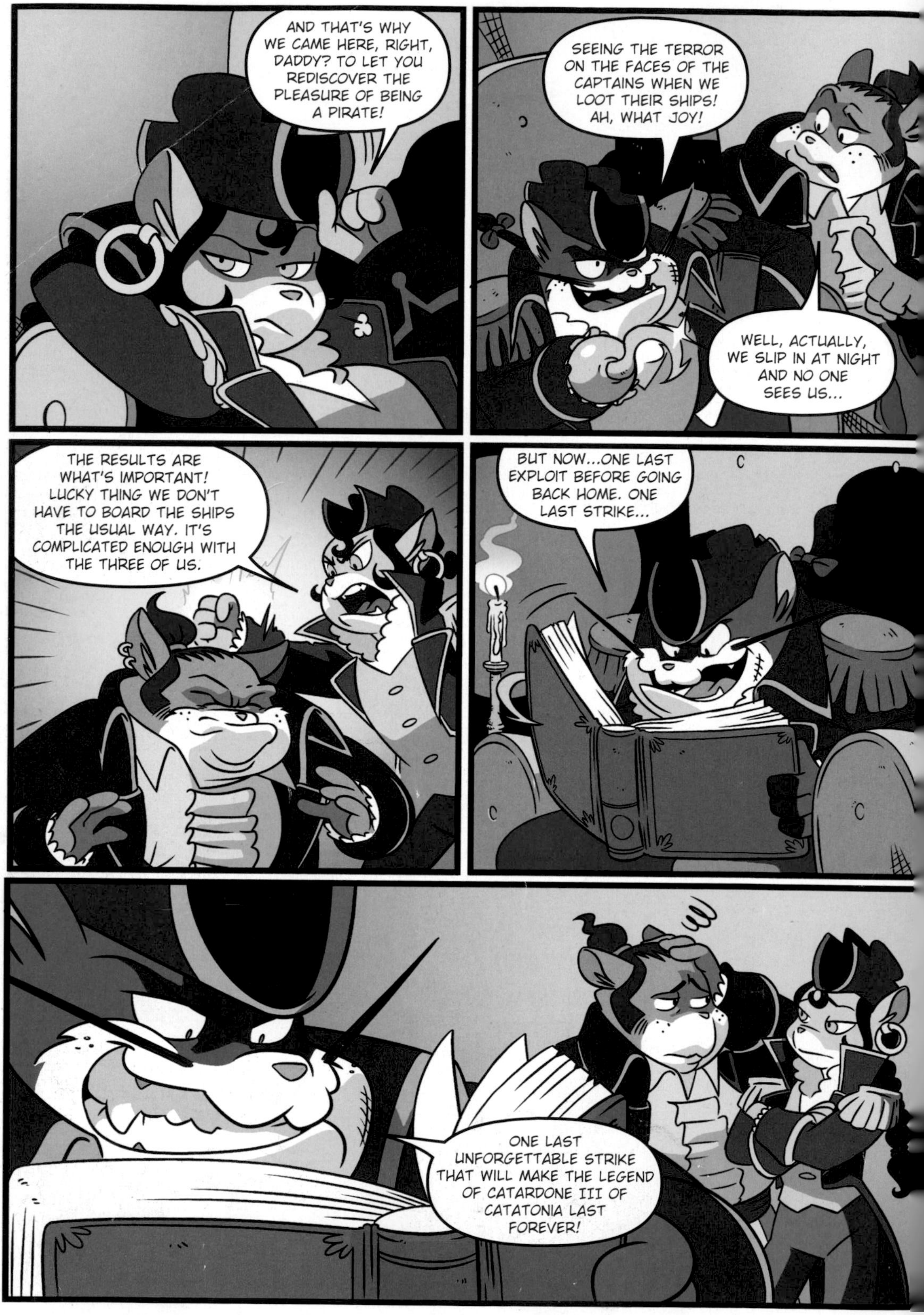
AND THAT'S WHY WE CAME HERE, RIGHT, DADDY? TO LET YOU REDISCOVER THE PLEASURE OF BEING A PIRATE!
SEEING THE TERROR ON THE FACES OF THE CAPTAINS WHEN WE LOOT THEIR SHIPS! AH, WHAT JOY!
WELL, ACTUALLY, WE SLIP IN AT NIGHT AND NO ONE SEES US...
THE RESULTS ARE WHAT'S IMPORTANT! LUCKY THING WE DON'T HAVE TO BOARD THE SHIPS THE USUAL WAY. IT'S COMPLICATED ENOUGH WITH THE THREE OF US.
BUT NOW...ONE LAST EXPLOIT BEFORE GOING BACK HOME. ONE LAST STRIKE...
ONE LAST UNFORGETTABLE STRIKE THAT WILL MAKE THE LEGEND OF CATARDONE III OF CATATONIA LAST FOREVER!

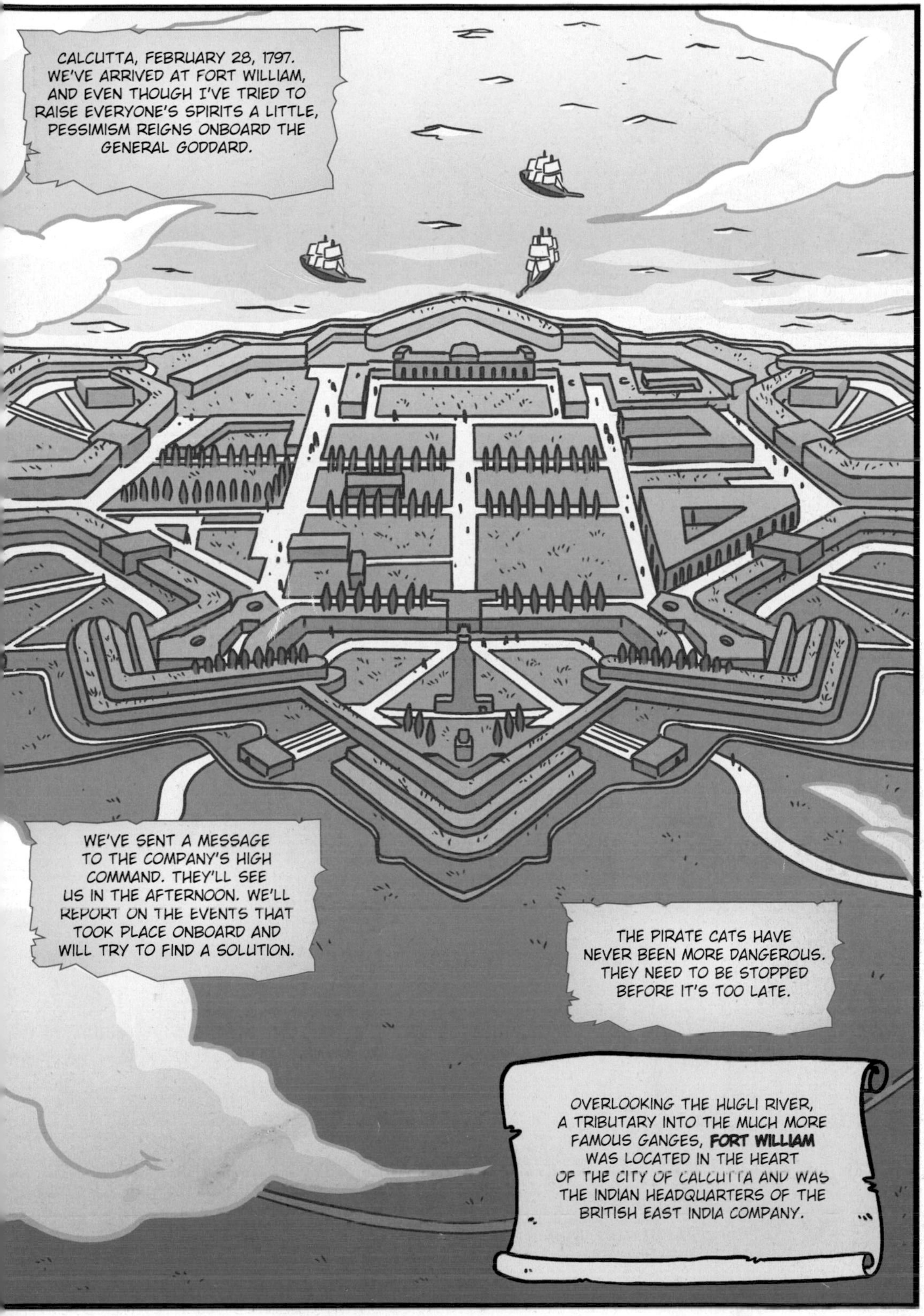
CALCUTTA, FEBRUARY 28, 1797. WE'VE ARRIVED AT FORT WILLIAM, AND EVEN THOUGH I'VE TRIED TO RAISE EVERYONE'S SPIRITS A LITTLE, PESSIMISM REIGNS ONBOARD THE GENERAL GODDARD.
WE'VE SENT A MESSAGE TO THE COMPANY'S HIGH COMMAND. THEY'LL SEE US IN THE AFTERNOON. WE'LL REPORT ON THE EVENTS THAT TOOK PLACE ONBOARD AND WILL TRY TO FIND A SOLUTION.
THE PIRATE CATS HAVE NEVER BEEN MORE DANGEROUS. THEY NEED TO BE STOPPED BEFORE IT'S TOO LATE.
OVERLOOKING THE HUGLI RIVER, A TRIBUTARY INTO THE MUCH MORE FAMOUS GANGES, **FORT WILLIAM** WAS LOCATED IN THE HEART OF THE CITY OF CALCUTTA AND WAS THE INDIAN HEADQUARTERS OF THE BRITISH EAST INDIA COMPANY.

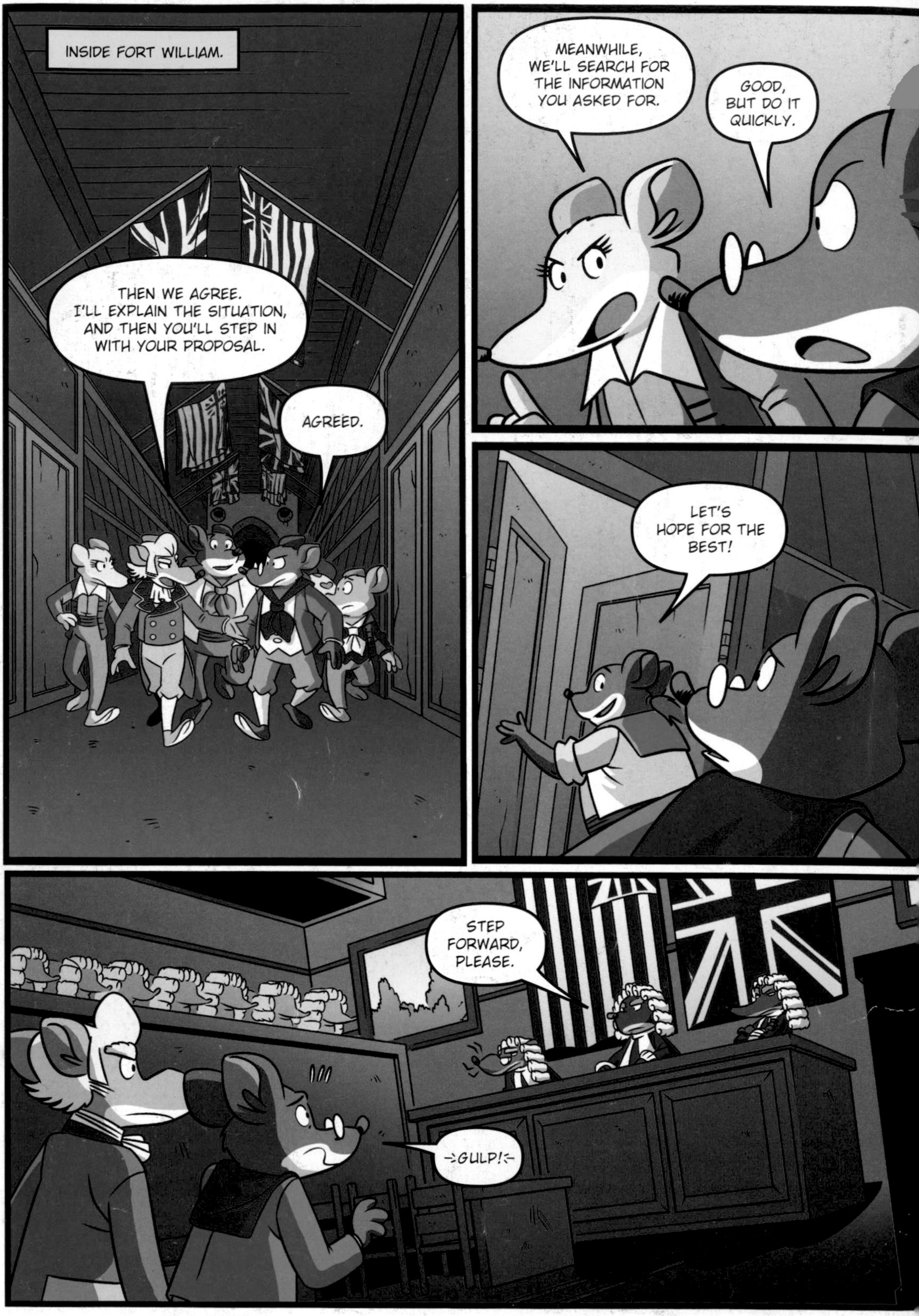
INSIDE FORT WILLIAM.
THEN WE AGREE. I'LL EXPLAIN THE SITUATION, AND THEN YOU'LL STEP IN WITH YOUR PROPOSAL.
AGREED.
MEANWHILE, WE'LL SEARCH FOR THE INFORMATION YOU ASKED FOR.
GOOD, BUT DO IT QUICKLY.
LET'S HOPE FOR THE BEST!
STEP FORWARD, PLEASE.
GULP!

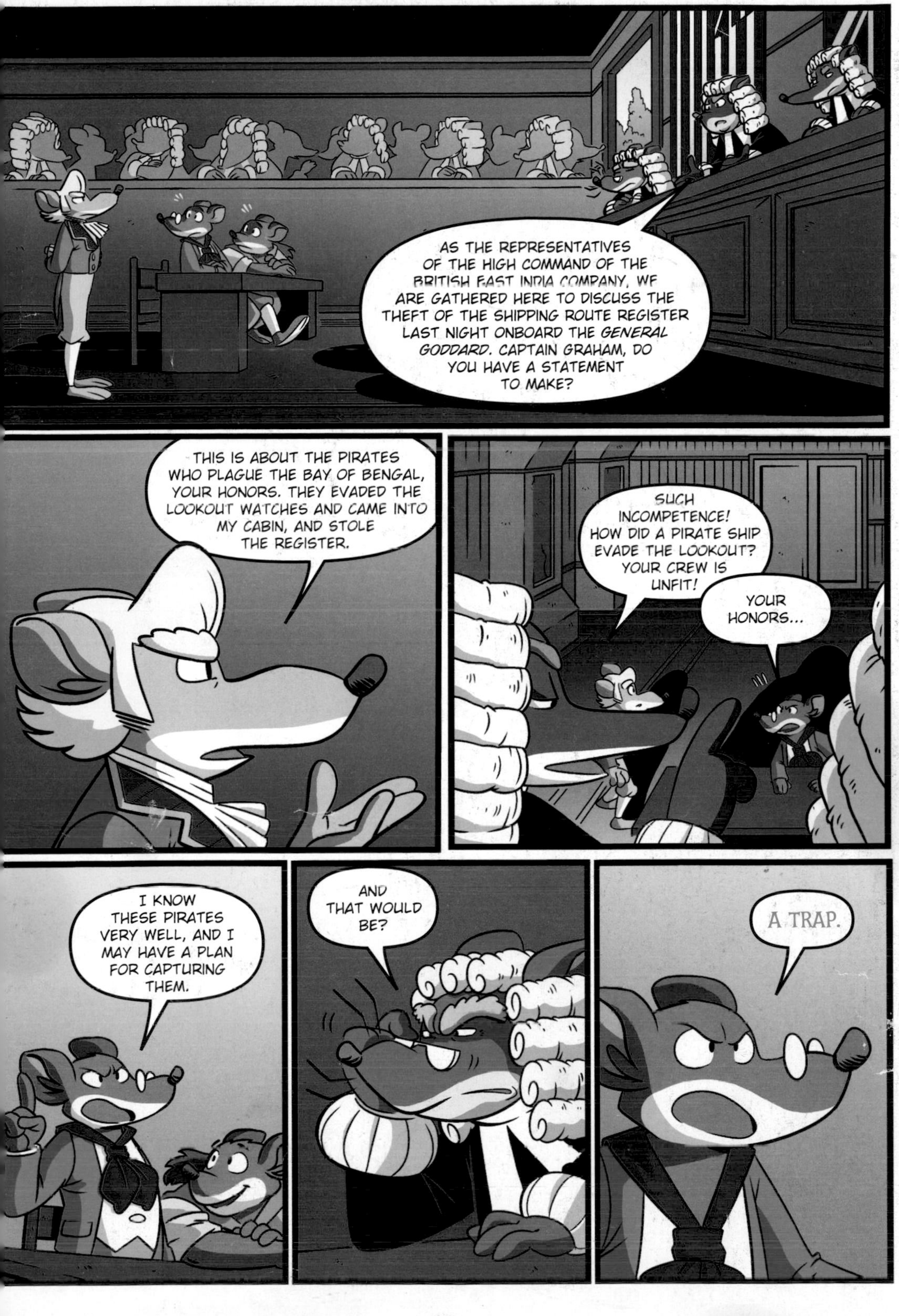
AS THE REPRESENTATIVES OF THE HIGH COMMAND OF THE BRITISH EAST INDIA COMPANY, WE ARE GATHERED HERE TO DISCUSS THE THEFT OF THE SHIPPING ROUTE REGISTER LAST NIGHT ONBOARD THE GENERAL GODDARD. CAPTAIN GRAHAM, DO YOU HAVE A STATEMENT TO MAKE?
THIS IS ABOUT THE PIRATES WHO PLAGUE THE BAY OF BENGAL, YOUR HONORS. THEY EVADED THE LOOKOUT WATCHES AND CAME INTO MY CABIN, AND STOLE THE REGISTER.
SUCH INCOMPETENCE! HOW DID A PIRATE SHIP EVADE THE LOOKOUT? YOUR CREW IS UNFIT!
YOUR HONORS...
I KNOW THESE PIRATES VERY WELL, AND I MAY HAVE A PLAN FOR CAPTURING THEM.
AND THAT WOULD BE?
A TRAP.

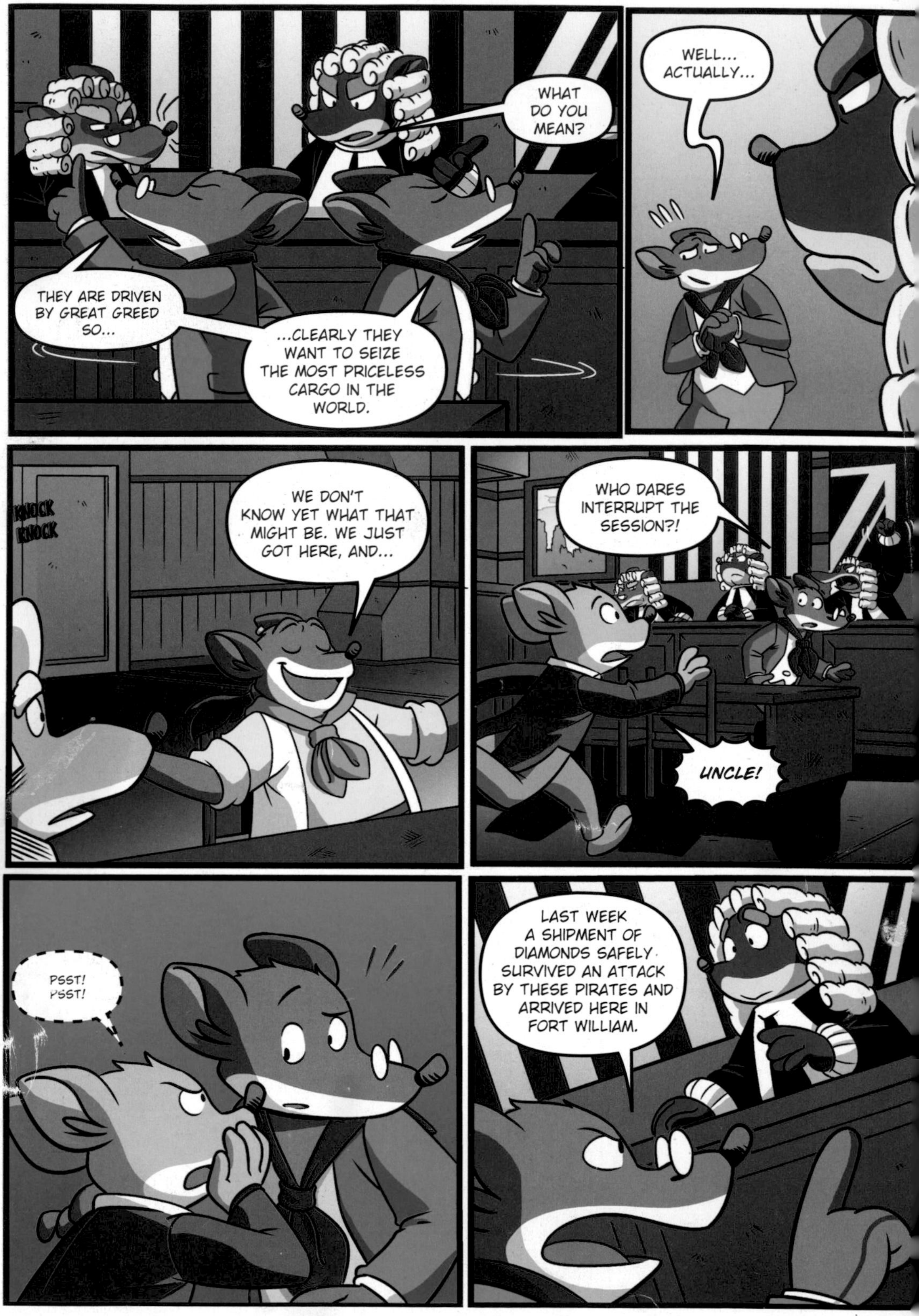
WHAT DO YOU MEAN?
THEY ARE DRIVEN BY GREAT GREED SO...
...CLEARLY THEY WANT TO SEIZE THE MOST PRICELESS CARGO IN THE WORLD.
WELL... ACTUALLY...
KNOCK KNOCK
WE DON'T KNOW YET WHAT THAT MIGHT BE. WE JUST GOT HERE, AND...
WHO DARES INTERRUPT THE SESSION?!
UNCLE!
PSST! PSST!
LAST WEEK A SHIPMENT OF DIAMONDS SAFELY SURVIVED AN ATTACK BY THESE PIRATES AND ARRIVED HERE IN FORT WILLIAM.

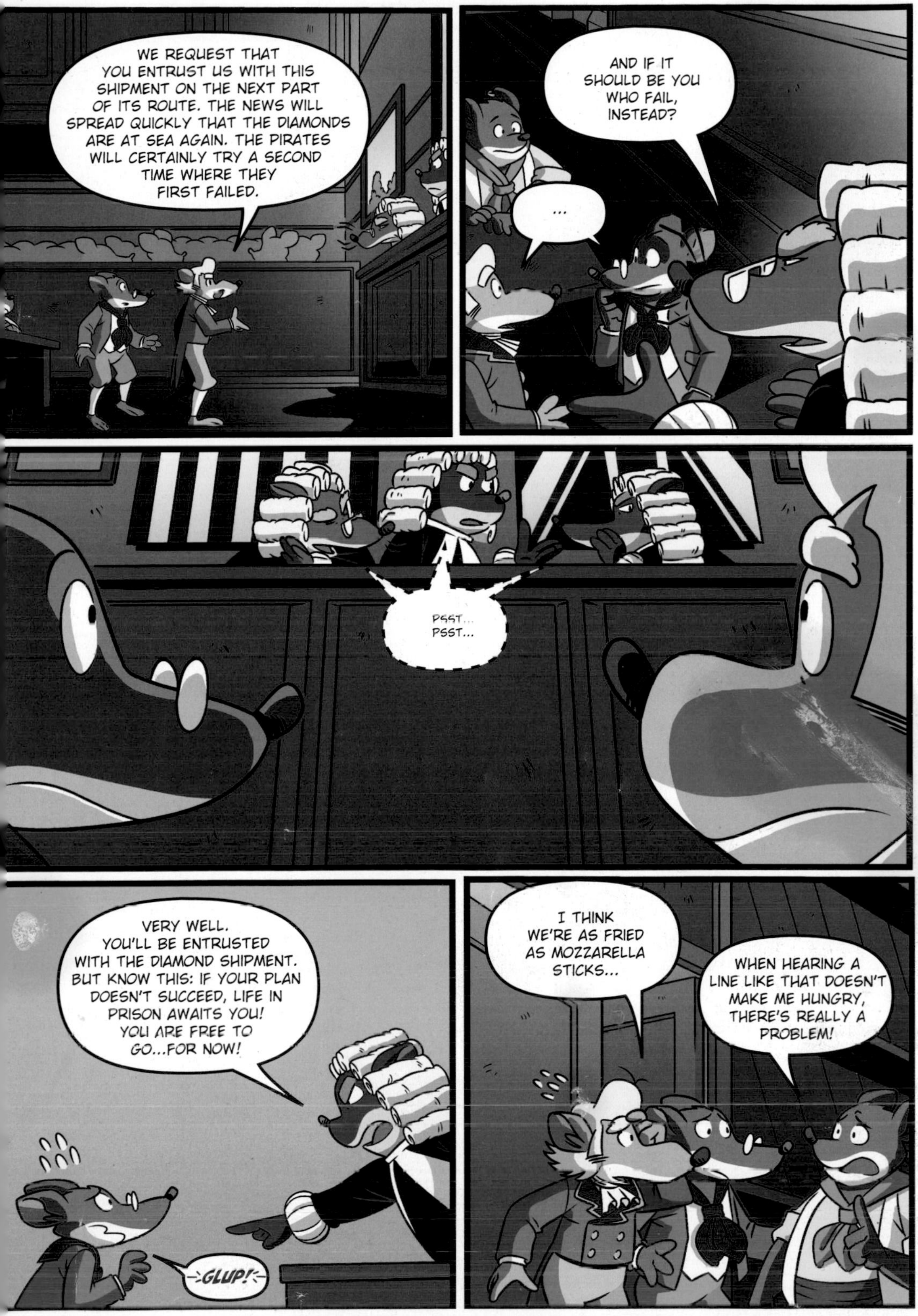
WE REQUEST THAT YOU ENTRUST US WITH THIS SHIPMENT ON THE NEXT PART OF ITS ROUTE. THE NEWS WILL SPREAD QUICKLY THAT THE DIAMONDS ARE AT SEA AGAIN. THE PIRATES WILL CERTAINLY TRY A SECOND TIME WHERE THEY FIRST FAILED.
AND IF IT SHOULD BE YOU WHO FAIL, INSTEAD?
...
PSST... PSST...
VERY WELL. YOU'LL BE ENTRUSTED WITH THE DIAMOND SHIPMENT. BUT KNOW THIS: IF YOUR PLAN DOESN'T SUCCEED, LIFE IN PRISON AWAITS YOU! YOU ARE FREE TO GO...FOR NOW!
GLUP!
I THINK WE'RE AS FRIED AS MOZZARELLA STICKS...
WHEN HEARING A LINE LIKE THAT DOESN'T MAKE ME HUNGRY, THERE'S REALLY A PROBLEM!

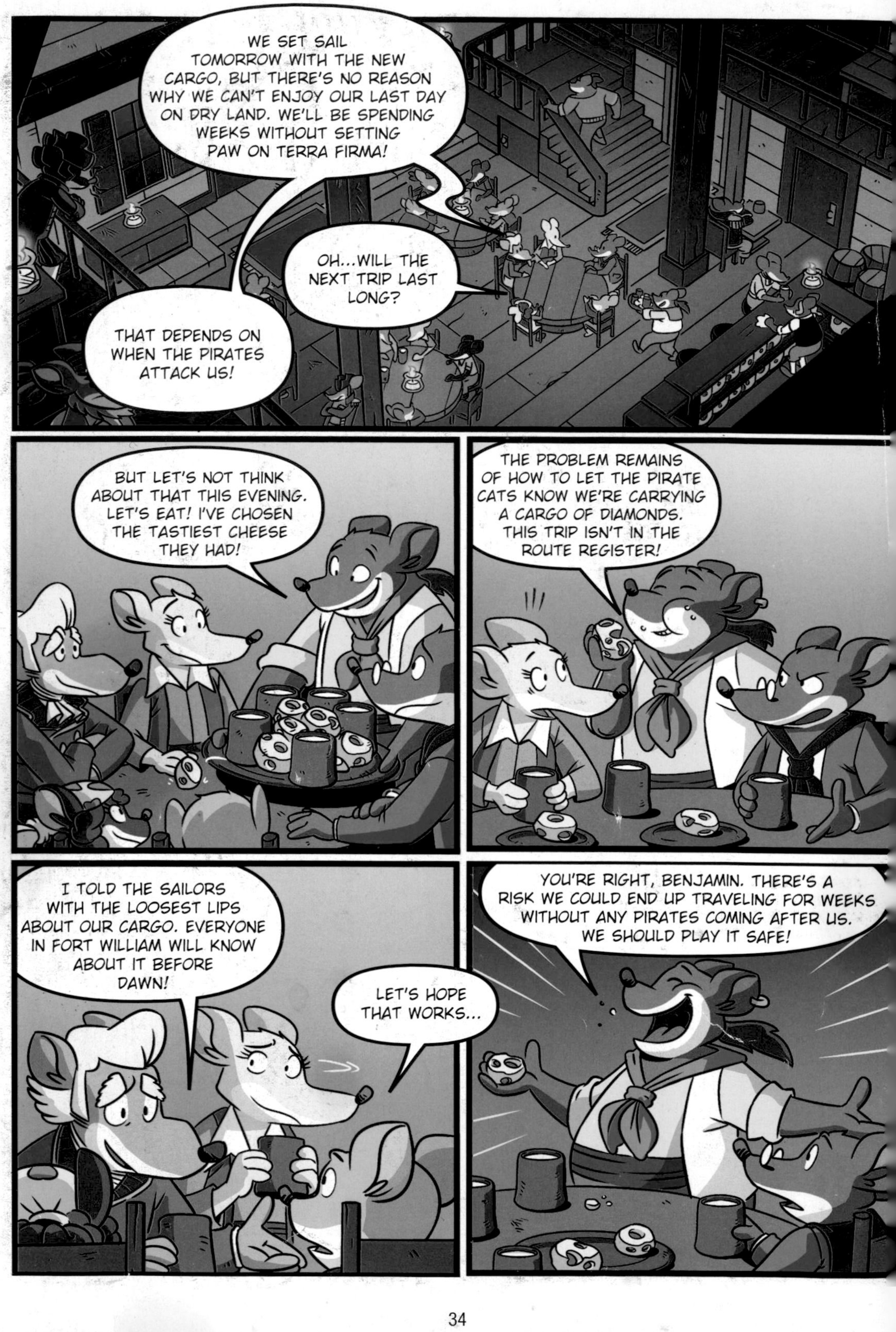
WE SET SAIL TOMORROW WITH THE NEW CARGO, BUT THERE'S NO REASON WHY WE CAN'T ENJOY OUR LAST DAY ON DRY LAND. WE'LL BE SPENDING WEEKS WITHOUT SETTING PAW ON TERRA FIRMA!
OH...WILL THE NEXT TRIP LAST LONG?
THAT DEPENDS ON WHEN THE PIRATES ATTACK US!
BUT LET'S NOT THINK ABOUT THAT THIS EVENING. LET'S EAT! I'VE CHOSEN THE TASTIEST CHEESE THEY HAD!
THE PROBLEM REMAINS OF HOW TO LET THE PIRATE CATS KNOW WE'RE CARRYING A CARGO OF DIAMONDS. THIS TRIP ISN'T IN THE ROUTE REGISTER!
I TOLD THE SAILORS WITH THE LOOSEST LIPS ABOUT OUR CARGO. EVERYONE IN FORT WILLIAM WILL KNOW ABOUT IT BEFORE DAWN!
LET'S HOPE THAT WORKS...
YOU'RE RIGHT, BENJAMIN. THERE'S A RISK WE COULD END UP TRAVELING FOR WEEKS WITHOUT ANY PIRATES COMING AFTER US. WE SHOULD PLAY IT SAFE!

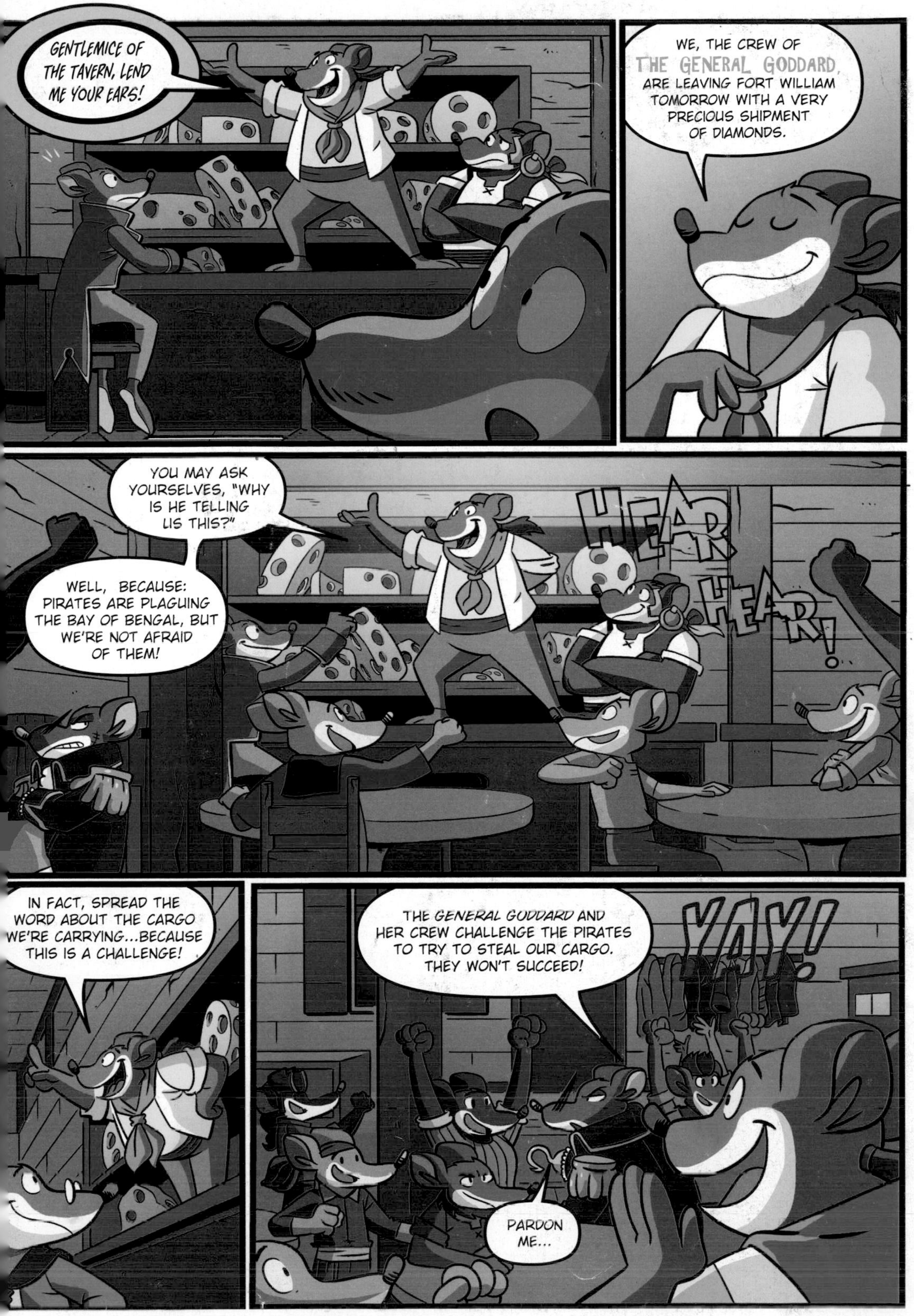
GENTLEMICE OF THE TAVERN, LEND ME YOUR EARS!
WE, THE CREW OF THE GENERAL GODDARD, ARE LEAVING FORT WILLIAM TOMORROW WITH A VERY PRECIOUS SHIPMENT OF DIAMONDS.
YOU MAY ASK YOURSELVES, "WHY IS HE TELLING US THIS?"
WELL, BECAUSE: PIRATES ARE PLAGUING THE BAY OF BENGAL, BUT WE'RE NOT AFRAID OF THEM!
HEAR HEAR!
IN FACT, SPREAD THE WORD ABOUT THE CARGO WE'RE CARRYING...BECAUSE THIS IS A CHALLENGE!
THE GENERAL GODDARD AND HER CREW CHALLENGE THE PIRATES TO TRY TO STEAL OUR CARGO. THEY WON'T SUCCEED!
YAY!
PARDON ME...

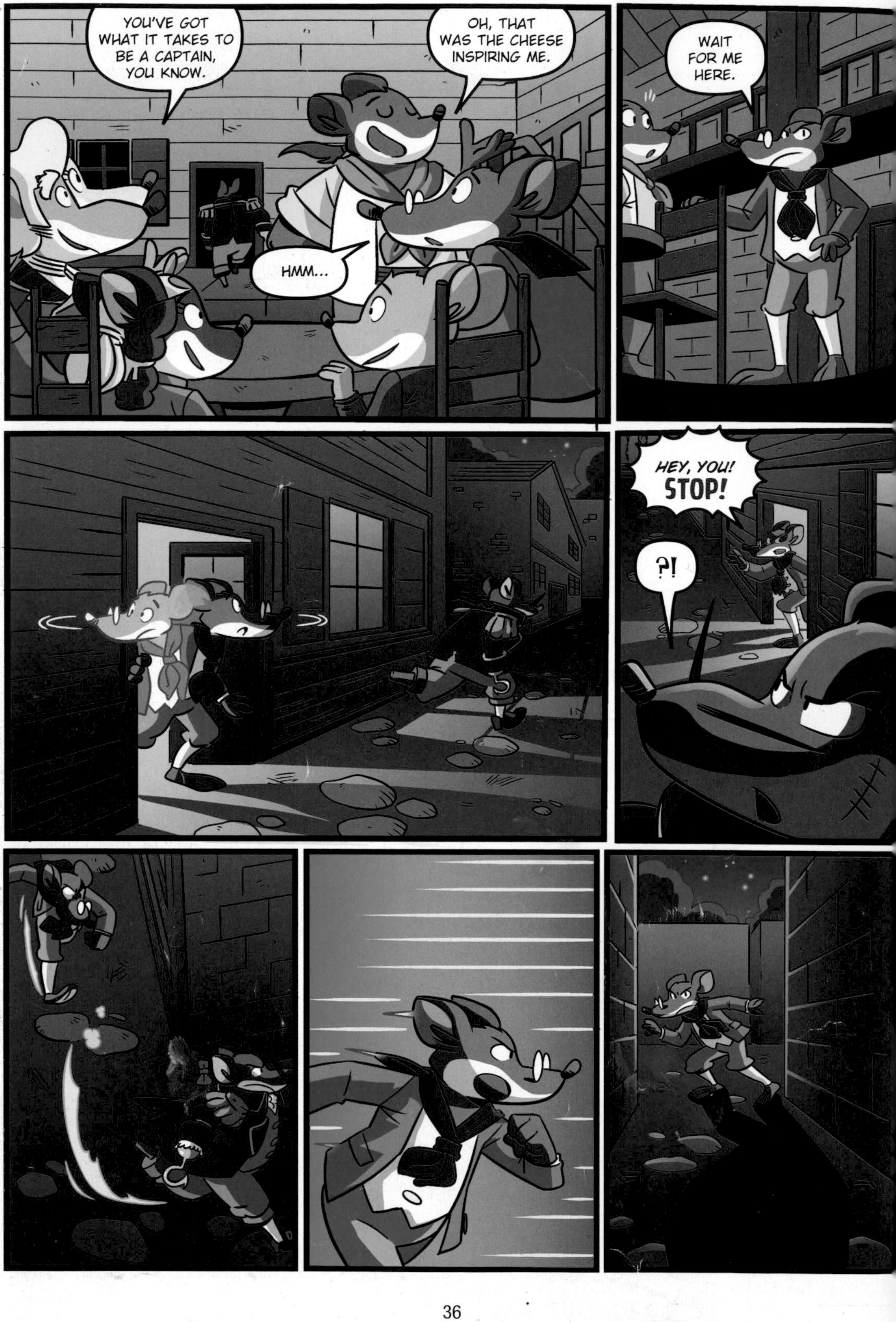
YOU'VE GOT WHAT IT TAKES TO BE A CAPTAIN, YOU KNOW.
OH, THAT WAS THE CHEESE INSPIRING ME.
HMM...
WAIT FOR ME HERE.
HEY, YOU! STOP!
?!

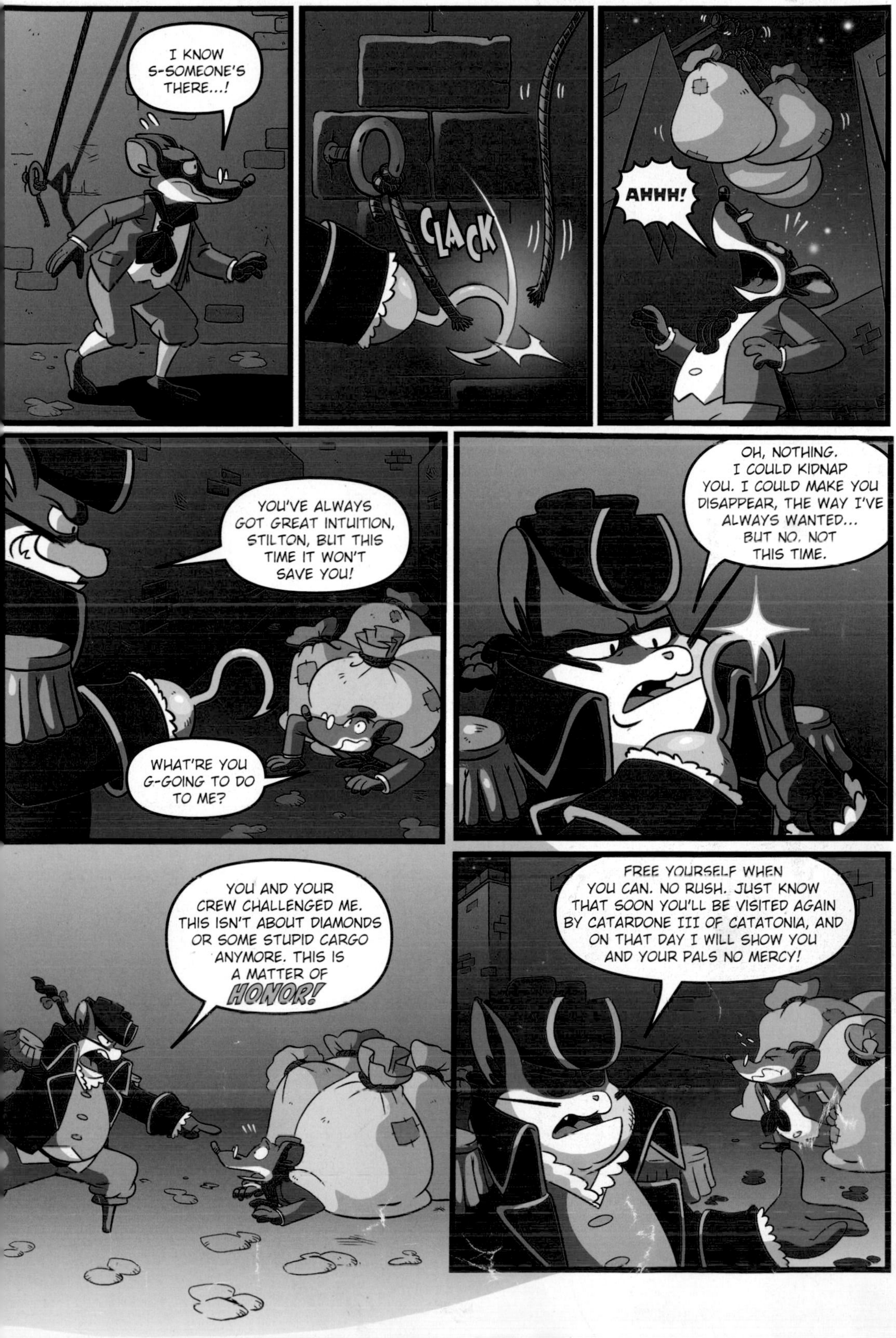
I KNOW S-SOMEONE'S THERE...!
CLACK
AHHH!
YOU'VE ALWAYS GOT GREAT INTUITION, STILTON, BUT THIS TIME IT WON'T SAVE YOU!
WHAT'RE YOU G-GOING TO DO TO ME?
OH, NOTHING. I COULD KIDNAP YOU. I COULD MAKE YOU DISAPPEAR, THE WAY I'VE ALWAYS WANTED... BUT NO. NOT THIS TIME.
YOU AND YOUR CREW CHALLENGED ME. THIS ISN'T ABOUT DIAMONDS OR SOME STUPID CARGO ANYMORE. THIS IS A MATTER OF HONOR!
FREE YOURSELF WHEN YOU CAN. NO RUSH. JUST KNOW THAT SOON YOU'LL BE VISITED AGAIN BY CATARDONE III OF CATATONIA, AND ON THAT DAY I WILL SHOW YOU AND YOUR PALS NO MERCY!

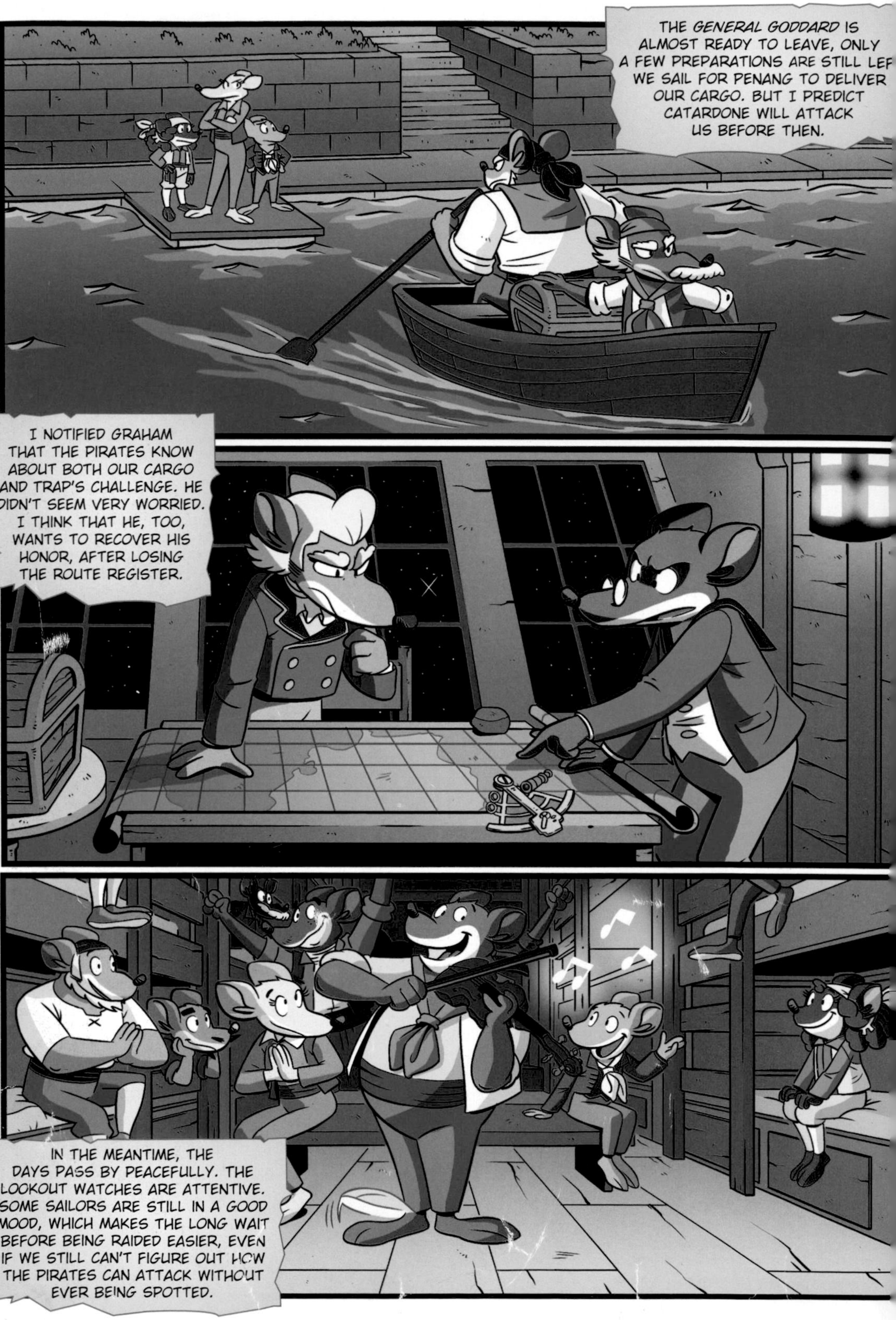
THE *GENERAL GODDARD* IS ALMOST READY TO LEAVE, ONLY A FEW PREPARATIONS ARE STILL LEF WE SAIL FOR PENANG TO DELIVER OUR CARGO. BUT I PREDICT CATARDONE WILL ATTACK US BEFORE THEN.
I NOTIFIED GRAHAM THAT THE PIRATES KNOW ABOUT BOTH OUR CARGO AND TRAP'S CHALLENGE. HE DIDN'T SEEM VERY WORRIED. I THINK THAT HE, TOO, WANTS TO RECOVER HIS HONOR, AFTER LOSING THE ROUTE REGISTER.
IN THE MEANTIME, THE DAYS PASS BY PEACEFULLY. THE LOOKOUT WATCHES ARE ATTENTIVE. SOME SAILORS ARE STILL IN A GOOD MOOD, WHICH MAKES THE LONG WAIT BEFORE BEING RAIDED EASIER, EVEN IF WE STILL CAN'T FIGURE OUT HOW THE PIRATES CAN ATTACK WITHOUT EVER BEING SPOTTED.

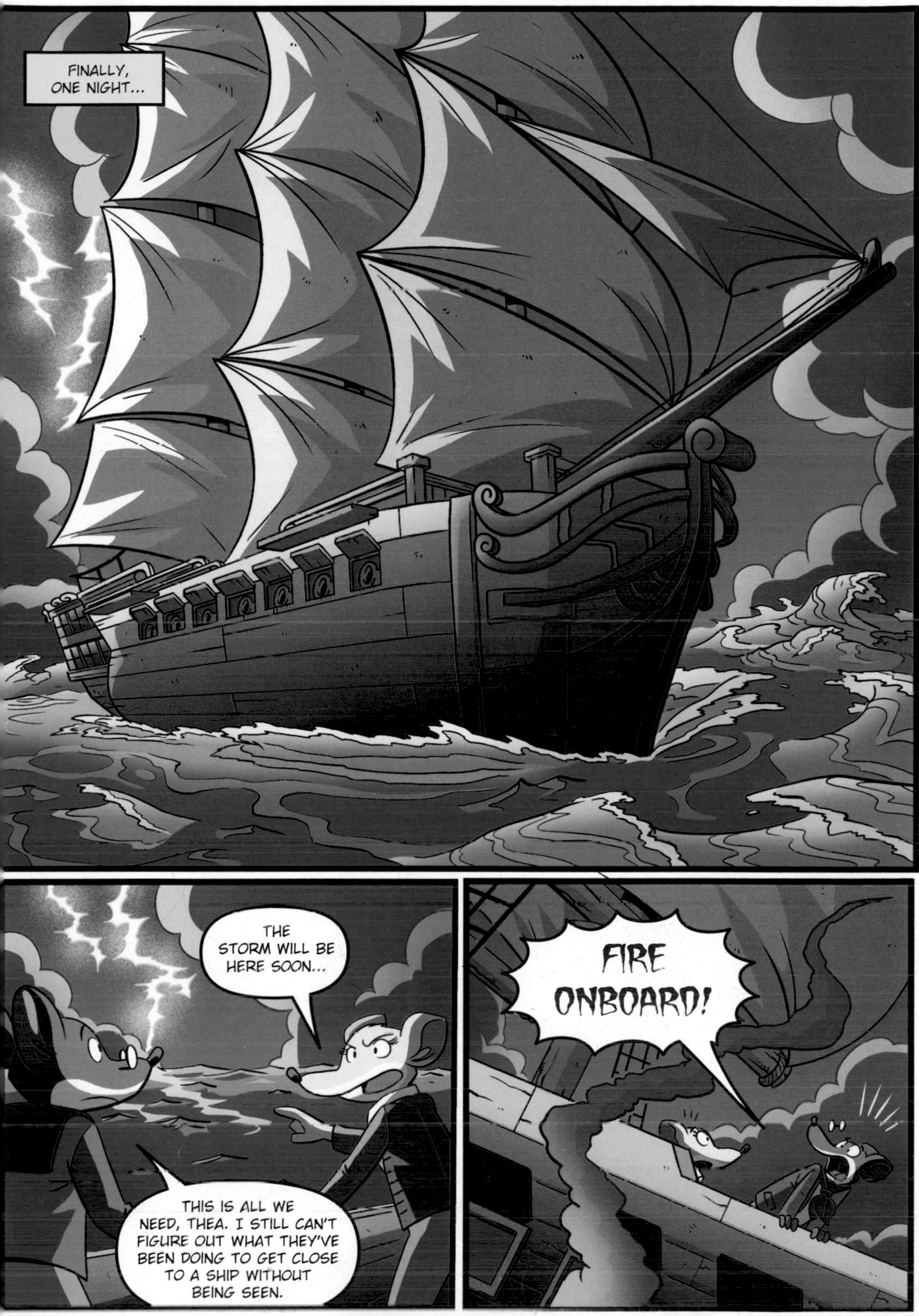
FINALLY, ONE NIGHT...
THE STORM WILL BE HERE SOON...
THIS IS ALL WE NEED, THEA. I STILL CAN'T FIGURE OUT WHAT THEY'VE BEEN DOING TO GET CLOSE TO A SHIP WITHOUT BEING SEEN.
FIRE ONBOARD!

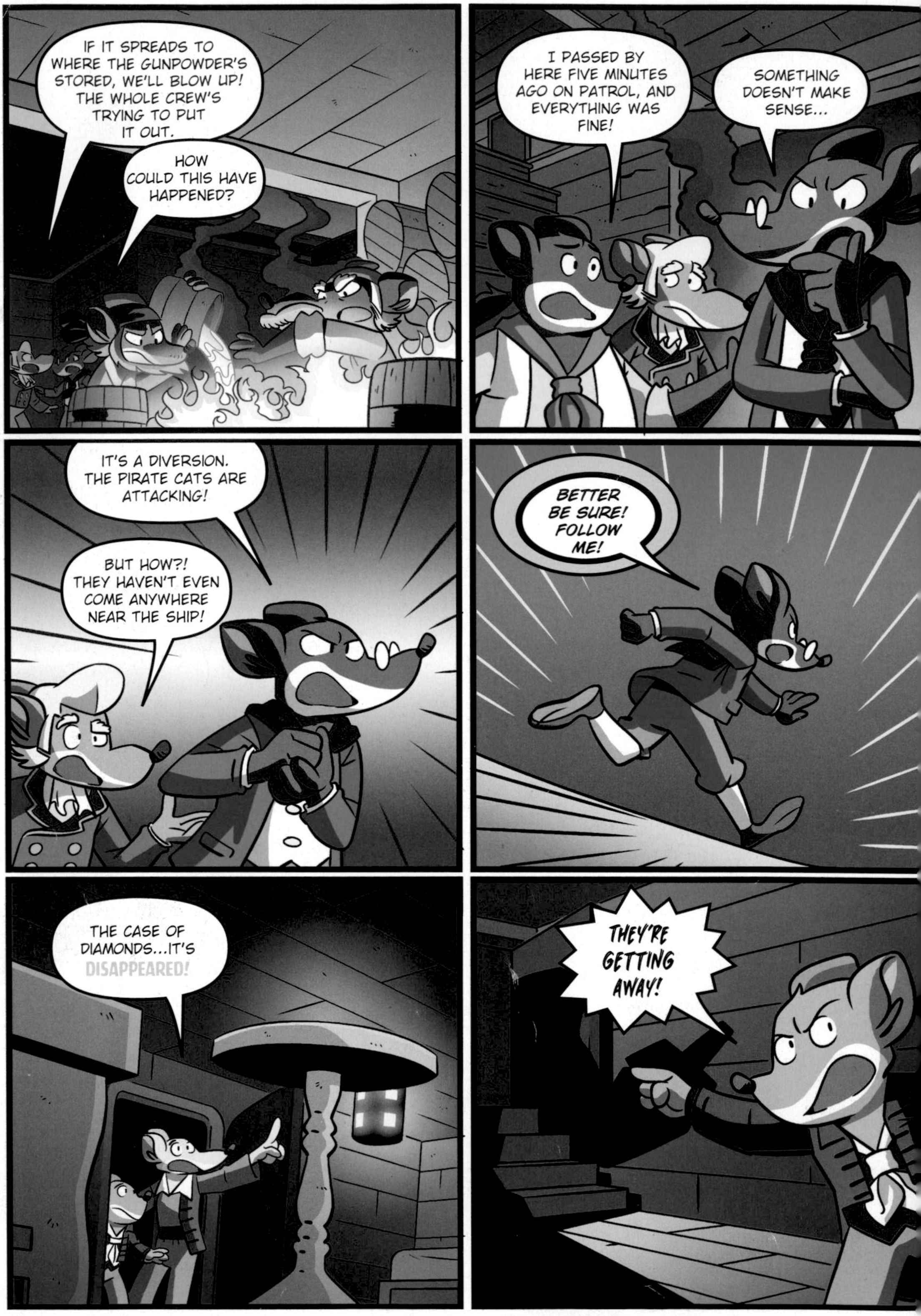
IF IT SPREADS TO WHERE THE GUNPOWDER'S STORED, WE'LL BLOW UP! THE WHOLE CREW'S TRYING TO PUT IT OUT.
HOW COULD THIS HAVE HAPPENED?
I PASSED BY HERE FIVE MINUTES AGO ON PATROL, AND EVERYTHING WAS FINE!
SOMETHING DOESN'T MAKE SENSE...
IT'S A DIVERSION. THE PIRATE CATS ARE ATTACKING!
BUT HOW?! THEY HAVEN'T EVEN COME ANYWHERE NEAR THE SHIP!
BETTER BE SURE! FOLLOW ME!
THE CASE OF DIAMONDS...IT'S DISAPPEARED!
THEY'RE GETTING AWAY!

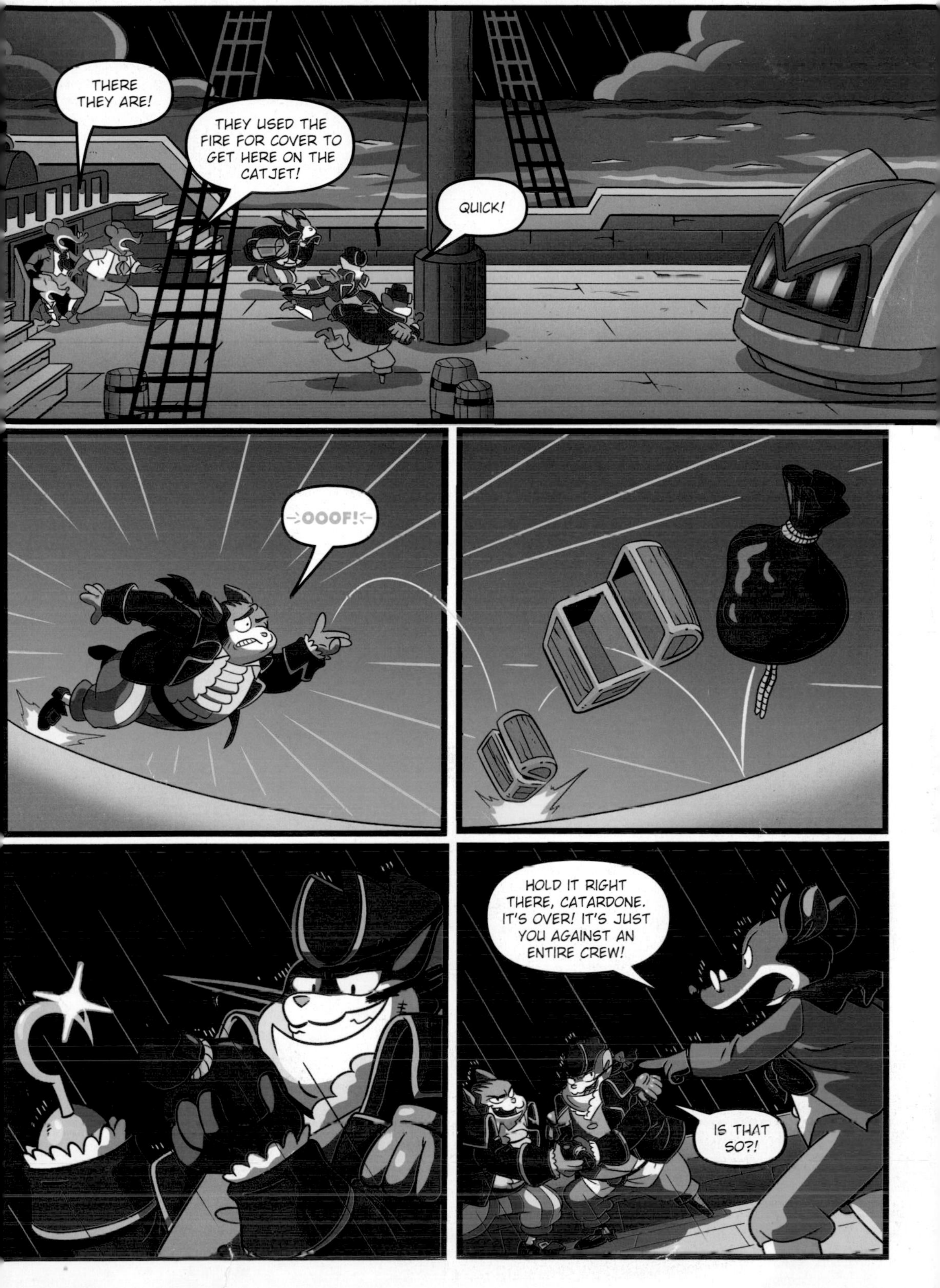
THERE THEY ARE!
THEY USED THE FIRE FOR COVER TO GET HERE ON THE CATJET!
QUICK!
OOOF!
HOLD IT RIGHT THERE, CATARDONE. IT'S OVER! IT'S JUST YOU AGAINST AN ENTIRE CREW!
IS THAT SO?!

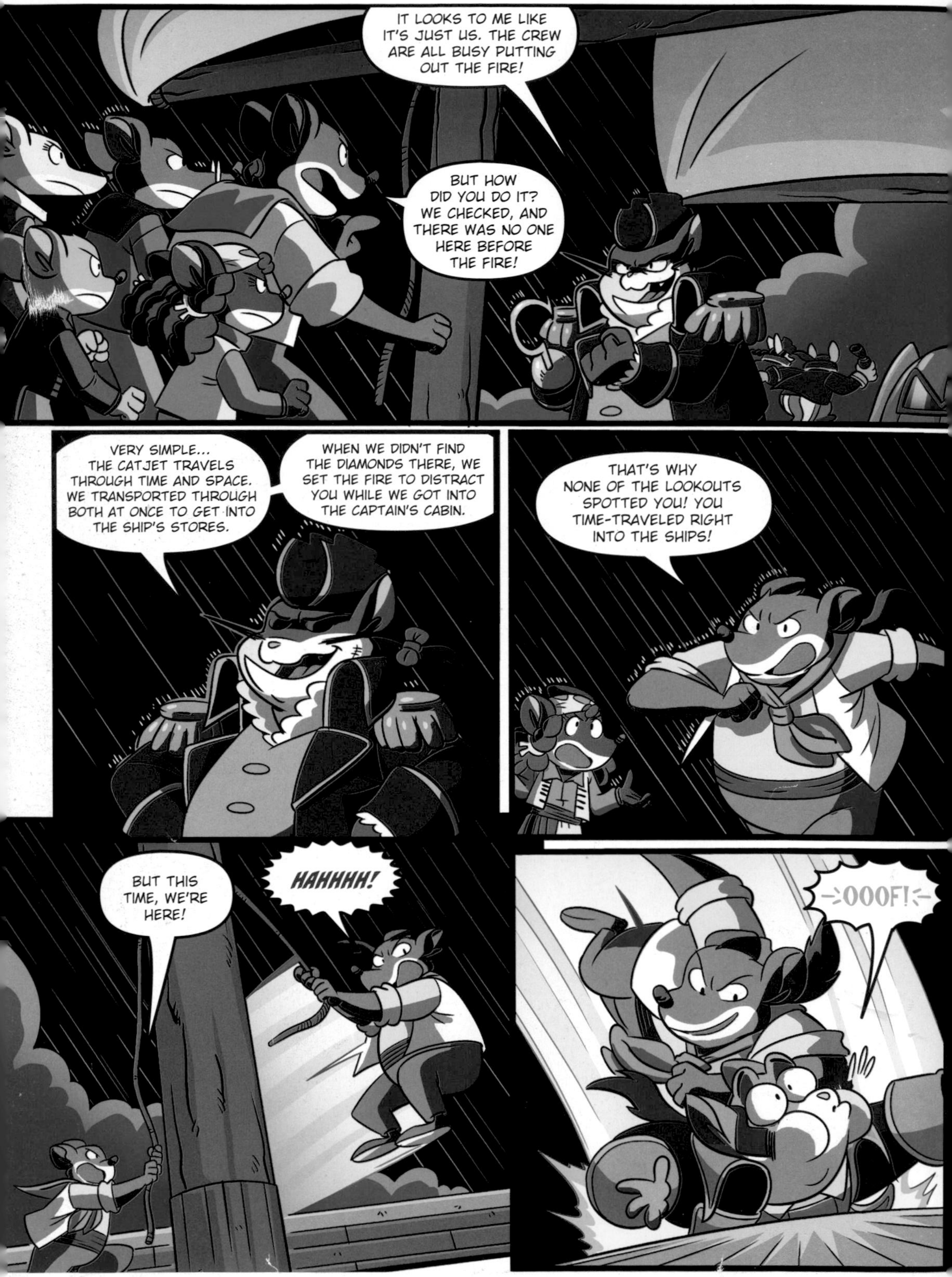
IT LOOKS TO ME LIKE IT'S JUST US. THE CREW ARE ALL BUSY PUTTING OUT THE FIRE!
BUT HOW DID YOU DO IT? WE CHECKED, AND THERE WAS NO ONE HERE BEFORE THE FIRE!
VERY SIMPLE... THE CATJET TRAVELS THROUGH TIME AND SPACE. WE TRANSPORTED THROUGH BOTH AT ONCE TO GET INTO THE SHIP'S STORES.
WHEN WE DIDN'T FIND THE DIAMONDS THERE, WE SET THE FIRE TO DISTRACT YOU WHILE WE GOT INTO THE CAPTAIN'S CABIN.
THAT'S WHY NONE OF THE LOOKOUTS SPOTTED YOU! YOU TIME-TRAVELED RIGHT INTO THE SHIPS!
BUT THIS TIME, WE'RE HERE!
HAHHHH!
OOOF!

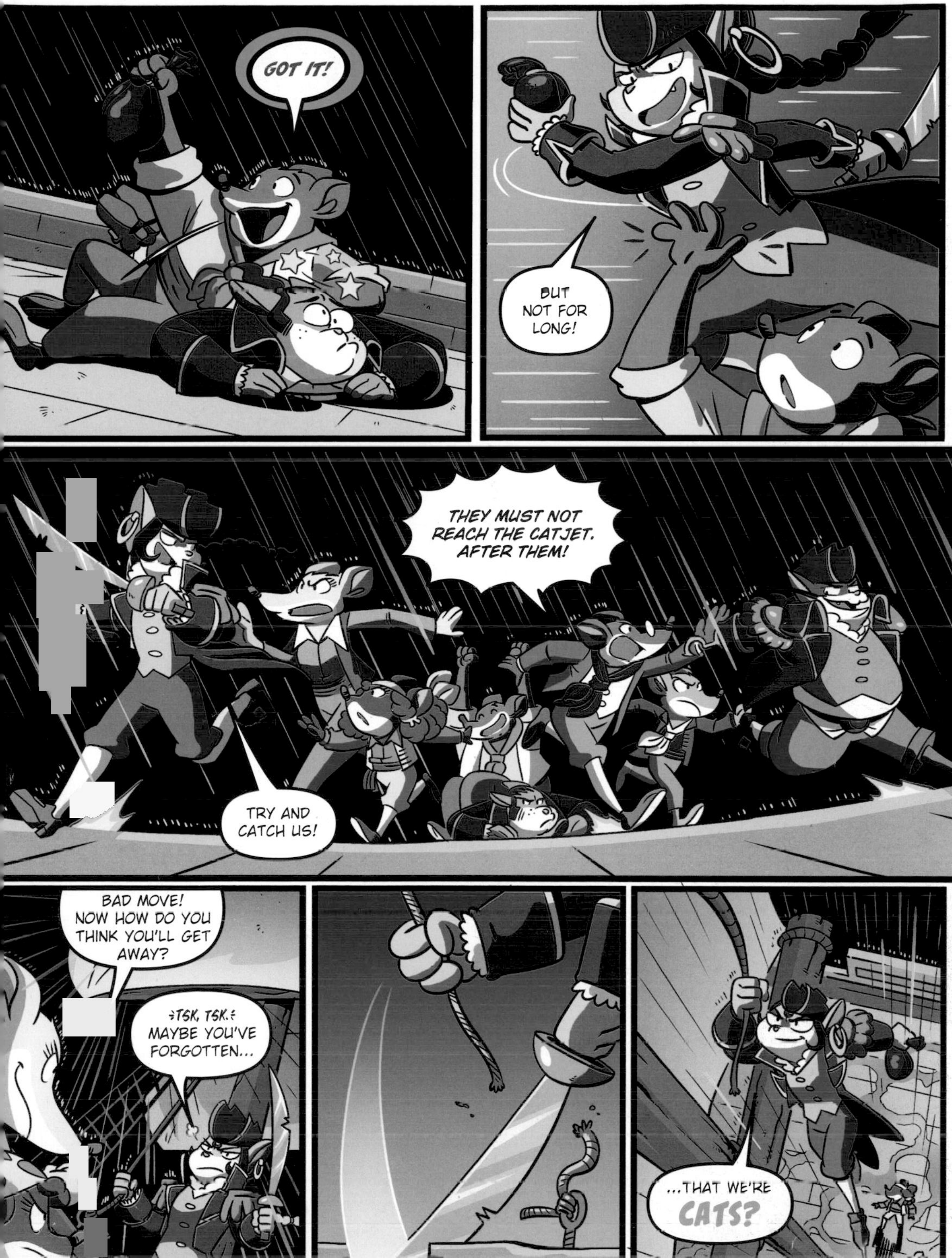
GOT IT!
BUT NOT FOR LONG!
THEY MUST NOT REACH THE CATJET. AFTER THEM!
TRY AND CATCH US!
BAD MOVE! NOW HOW DO YOU THINK YOU'LL GET AWAY?
TSK, TSK. MAYBE YOU'VE FORGOTTEN...
...THAT WE'RE CATS?

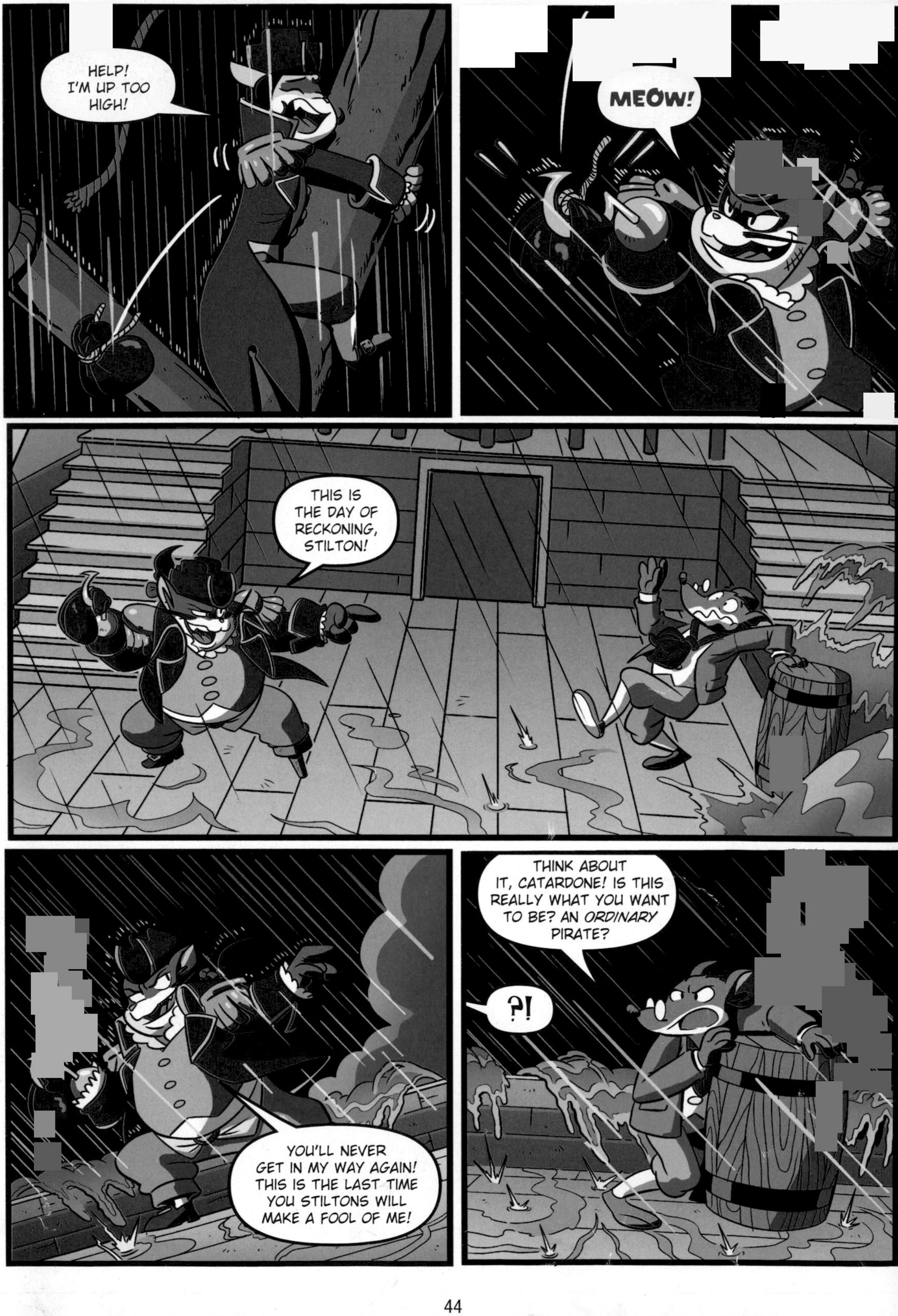
HELP! I'M UP TOO HIGH!
MEOW!
THIS IS THE DAY OF RECKONING, STILTON!
YOU'LL NEVER GET IN MY WAY AGAIN! THIS IS THE LAST TIME YOU STILTONS WILL MAKE A FOOL OF ME!
THINK ABOUT IT, CATARDONE! IS THIS REALLY WHAT YOU WANT TO BE? AN *ORDINARY* PIRATE?
?!

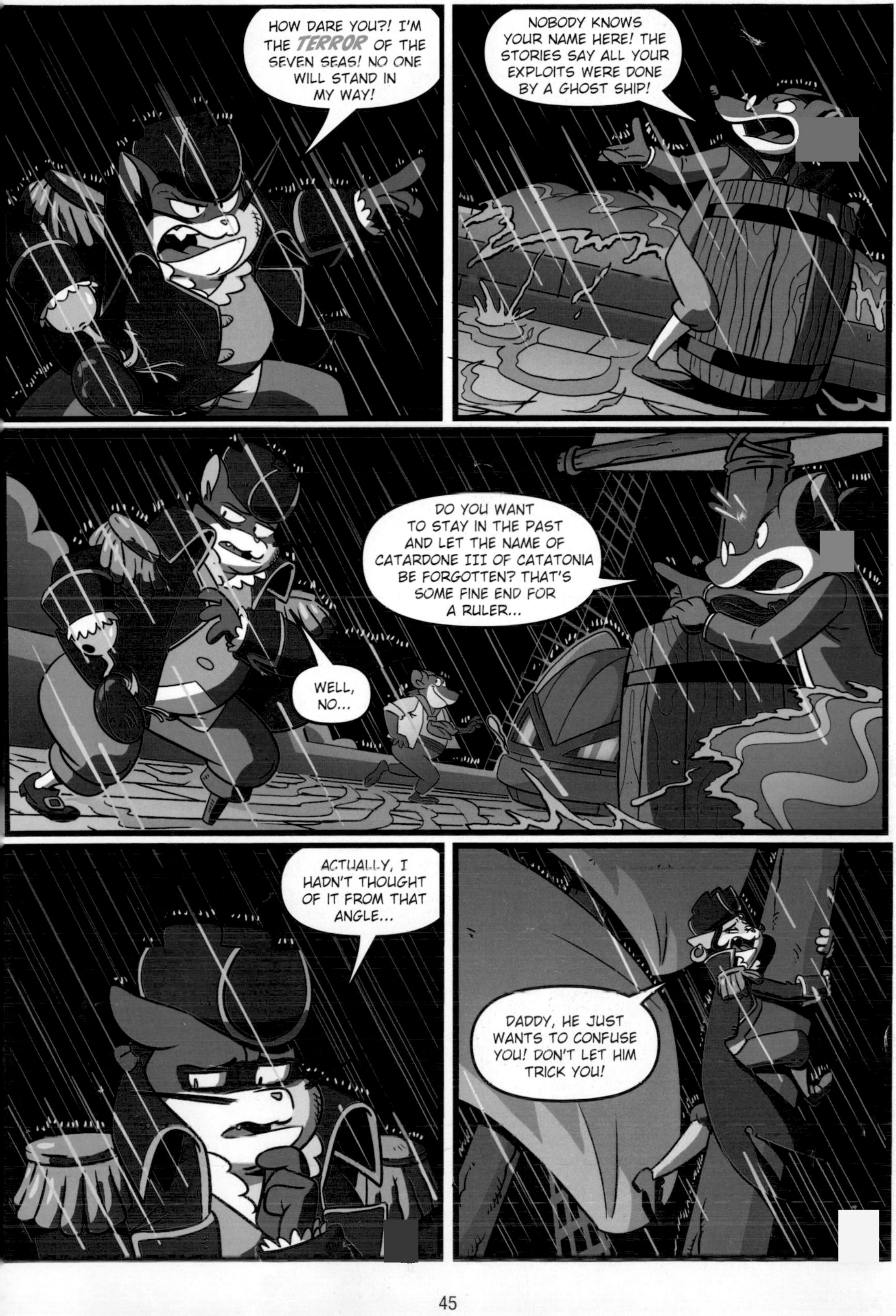
HOW DARE YOU?! I'M THE TERROR OF THE SEVEN SEAS! NO ONE WILL STAND IN MY WAY!
NOBODY KNOWS YOUR NAME HERE! THE STORIES SAY ALL YOUR EXPLOITS WERE DONE BY A GHOST SHIP!
DO YOU WANT TO STAY IN THE PAST AND LET THE NAME OF CATARDONE III OF CATATONIA BE FORGOTTEN? THAT'S SOME FINE END FOR A RULER...
WELL, NO...
ACTUALLY, I HADN'T THOUGHT OF IT FROM THAT ANGLE...
DADDY, HE JUST WANTS TO CONFUSE YOU! DON'T LET HIM TRICK YOU!

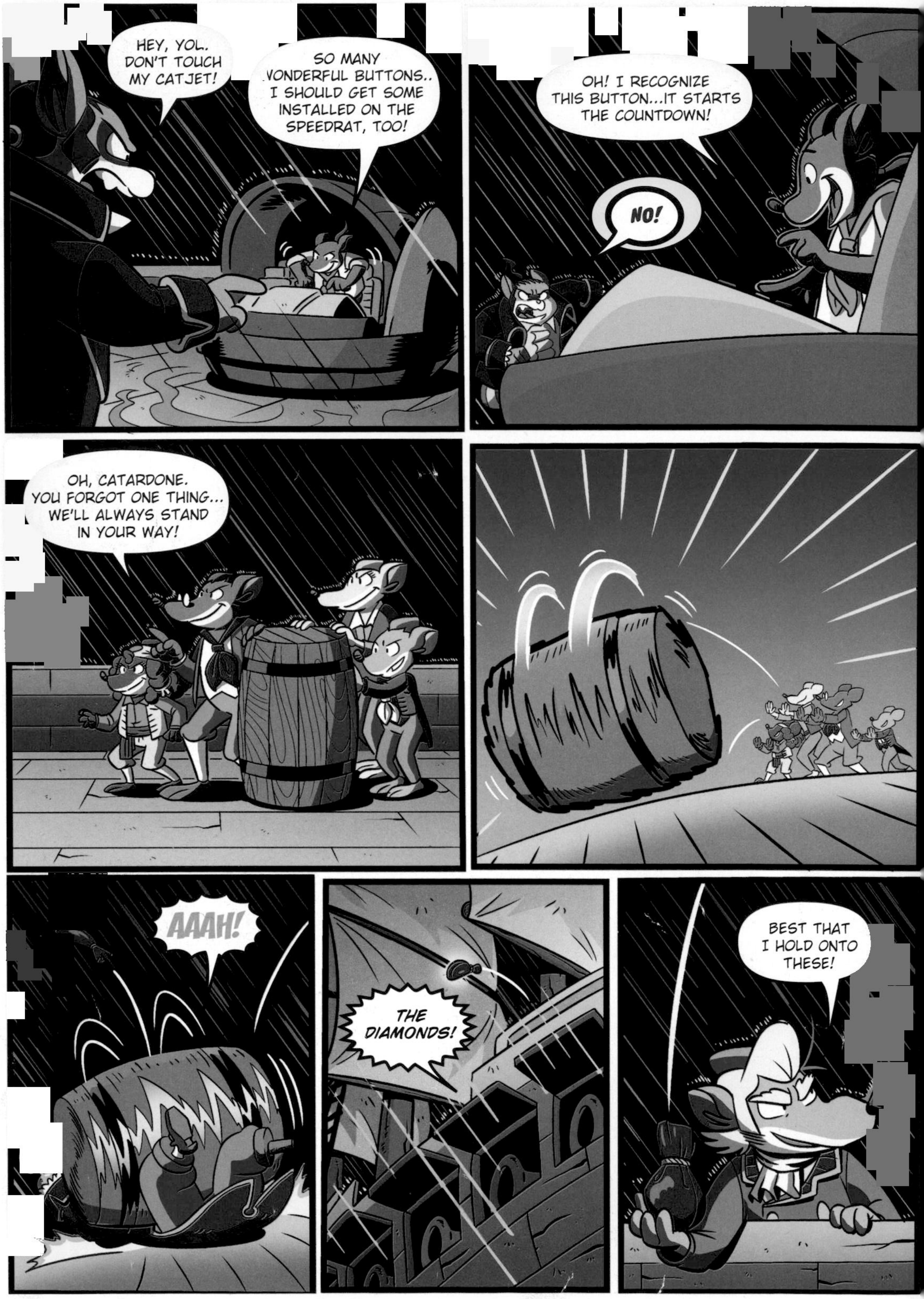
HEY, YOU. DON'T TOUCH MY CATJET!
SO MANY WONDERFUL BUTTONS.. I SHOULD GET SOME INSTALLED ON THE SPEEDRAT, TOO!
OH! I RECOGNIZE THIS BUTTON...IT STARTS THE COUNTDOWN!
NO!
OH, CATARDONE. YOU FORGOT ONE THING... WE'LL ALWAYS STAND IN YOUR WAY!
AAAH!
THE DIAMONDS!
BEST THAT I HOLD ONTO THESE!

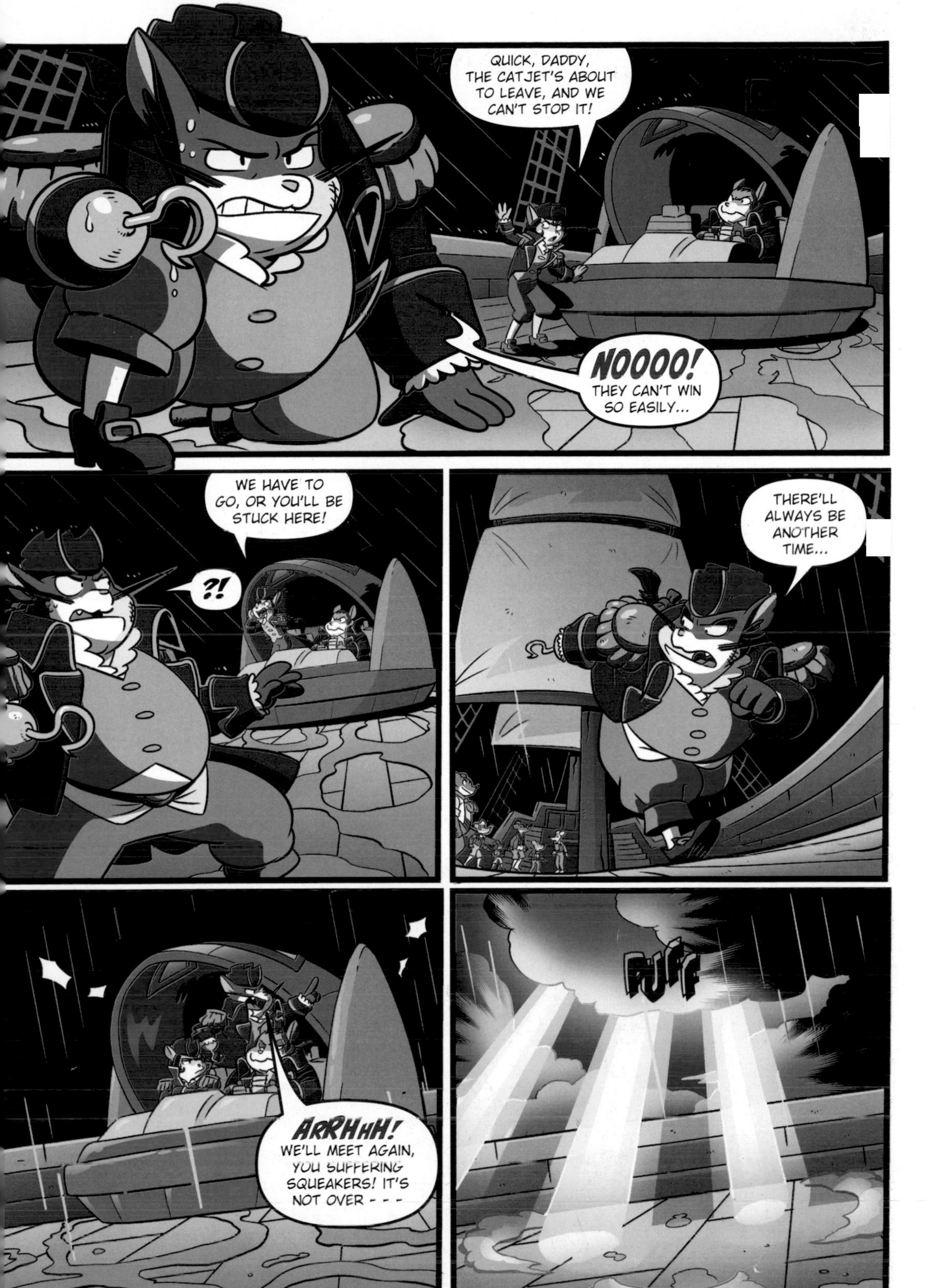
QUICK, DADDY, THE CATJET'S ABOUT TO LEAVE, AND WE CAN'T STOP IT!
NOOOO! THEY CAN'T WIN SO EASILY...
WE HAVE TO GO, OR YOU'LL BE STUCK HERE!
?!
THERE'LL ALWAYS BE ANOTHER TIME...
ARRHHH! WE'LL MEET AGAIN, YOU SUFFERING SQUEAKERS! IT'S NOT OVER - - -
PUFF

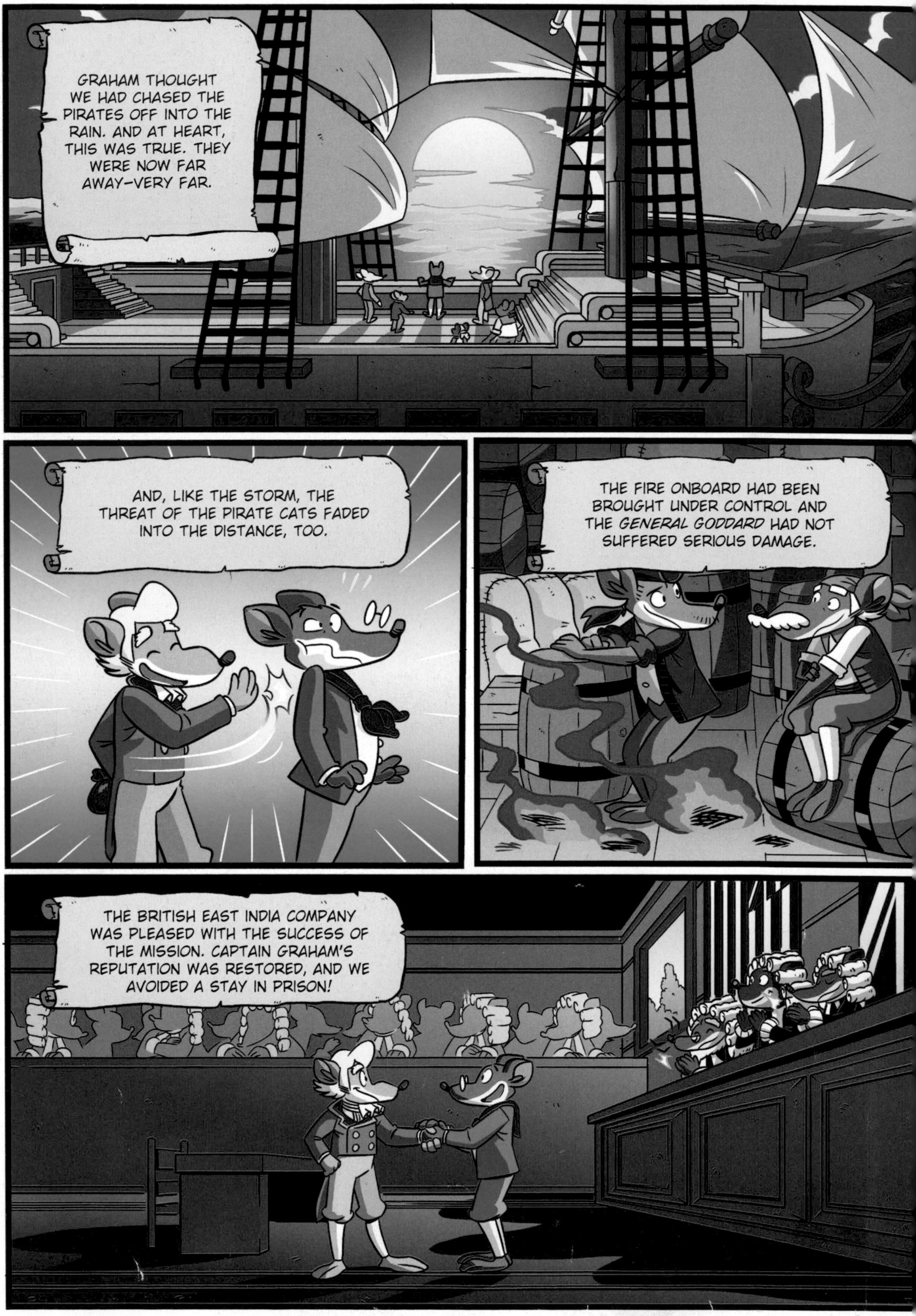
GRAHAM THOUGHT WE HAD CHASED THE PIRATES OFF INTO THE RAIN. AND AT HEART, THIS WAS TRUE. THEY WERE NOW FAR AWAY—VERY FAR.
AND, LIKE THE STORM, THE THREAT OF THE PIRATE CATS FADED INTO THE DISTANCE, TOO.
THE FIRE ONBOARD HAD BEEN BROUGHT UNDER CONTROL AND THE *GENERAL GODDARD* HAD NOT SUFFERED SERIOUS DAMAGE.
THE BRITISH EAST INDIA COMPANY WAS PLEASED WITH THE SUCCESS OF THE MISSION. CAPTAIN GRAHAM'S REPUTATION WAS RESTORED, AND WE AVOIDED A STAY IN PRISON!

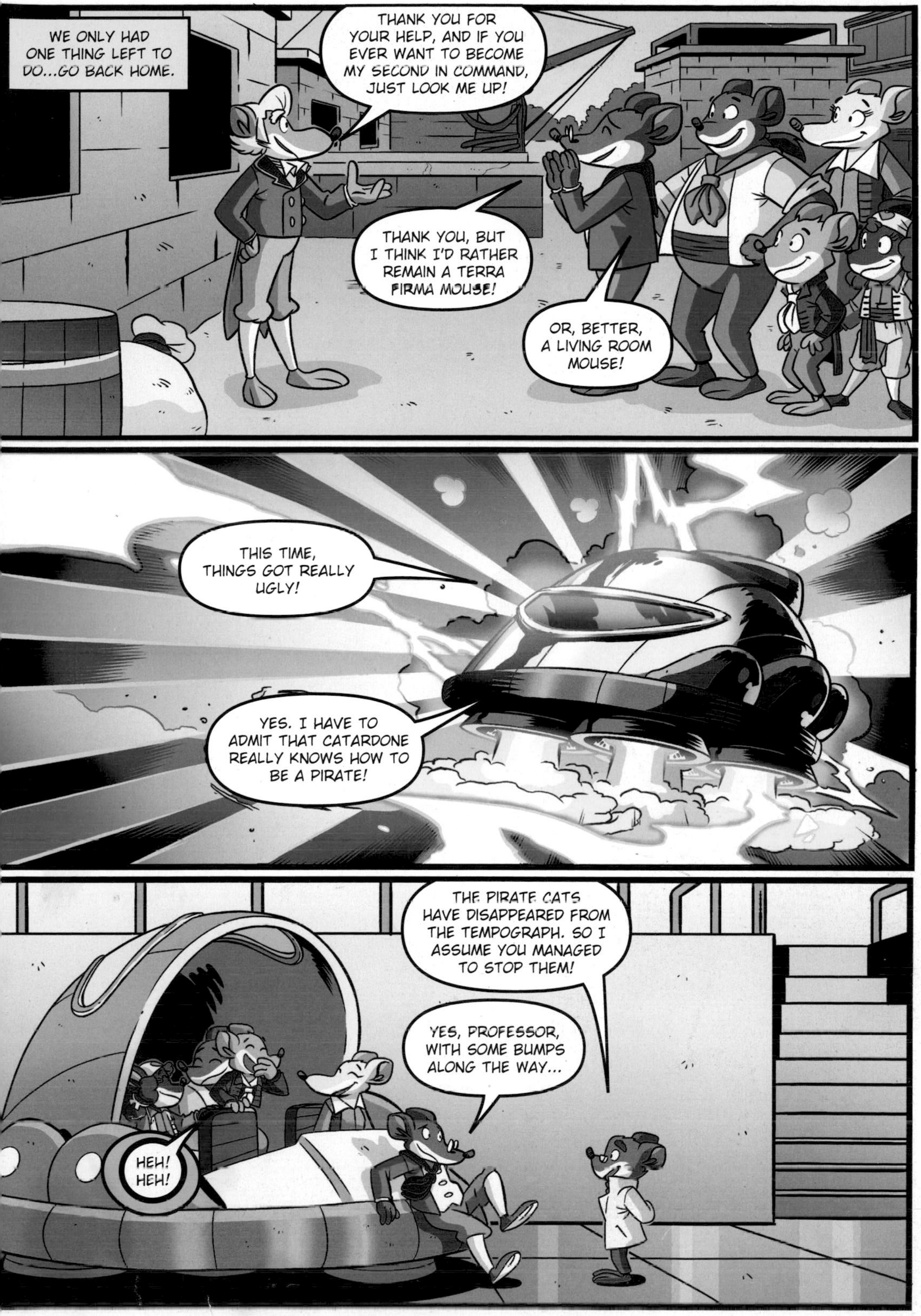
WE ONLY HAD ONE THING LEFT TO DO...GO BACK HOME.
THANK YOU FOR YOUR HELP, AND IF YOU EVER WANT TO BECOME MY SECOND IN COMMAND, JUST LOOK ME UP!
THANK YOU, BUT I THINK I'D RATHER REMAIN A TERRA FIRMA MOUSE!
OR, BETTER, A LIVING ROOM MOUSE!
THIS TIME, THINGS GOT REALLY UGLY!
YES. I HAVE TO ADMIT THAT CATARDONE REALLY KNOWS HOW TO BE A PIRATE!
THE PIRATE CATS HAVE DISAPPEARED FROM THE TEMPOGRAPH. SO I ASSUME YOU MANAGED TO STOP THEM!
YES, PROFESSOR, WITH SOME BUMPS ALONG THE WAY...
HEH! HEH!

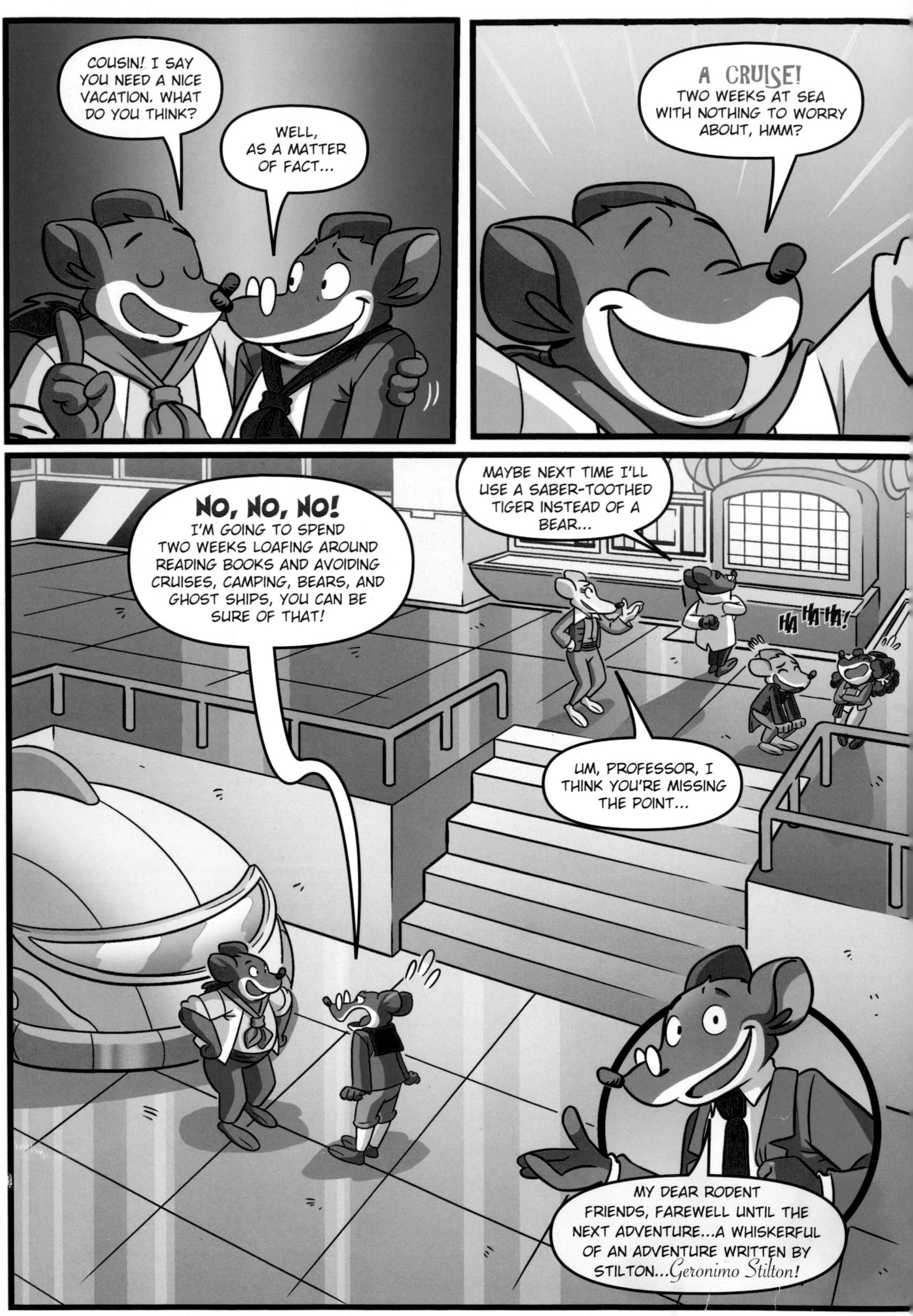
COUSIN! I SAY YOU NEED A NICE VACATION. WHAT DO YOU THINK?
WELL, AS A MATTER OF FACT...
A CRUISE! TWO WEEKS AT SEA WITH NOTHING TO WORRY ABOUT, HMM?
NO, NO, NO! I'M GOING TO SPEND TWO WEEKS LOAFING AROUND READING BOOKS AND AVOIDING CRUISES, CAMPING, BEARS, AND GHOST SHIPS, YOU CAN BE SURE OF THAT!
MAYBE NEXT TIME I'LL USE A SABER-TOOTHED TIGER INSTEAD OF A BEAR...
HA HA HA!
UM, PROFESSOR, I THINK YOU'RE MISSING THE POINT...
MY DEAR RODENT FRIENDS, FAREWELL UNTIL THE NEXT ADVENTURE...A WHISKERFUL OF AN ADVENTURE WRITTEN BY STILTON...Geronimo Stilton!

Watch Out For
PAPERCUTZ™

Welcome to the swashbuckling, sea-faring, seventeenth GERONIMO STILTON graphic novel, by Leonardo Favia, Francesco Savino, and Ryan Jampole—from Papercutz, those landlubbers dedicated to publishing great graphic novels for all ages. I'm Salicrup, *Jim Salicrup*, the Editor-in-Chief and Chief Deck-Swabber. If you're looking at a digital edition of this graphic novel, we hope it's an authorized version and not a . . . ahem . . . pirated edition.

For all you sharp-eyed Geronimo Stilton fans who carefully study page 4—the copyright page—of each GERONIMO STILTON graphic novel, you'll already know that starting from our first graphic novel we've been republishing material that was created and originally published in Italy. That's not uncommon for Papercutz; we publish English-language editions of many European graphic novels—THE SMURFS, DISNEY FAIRIES, THE SISTERS, ARIOL, DANCE CLASS, just to name a few. But something happened recently: We ran out of GERONIMO STILTON graphic novels. We published every single one that had been produced in Italy, and there weren't any left!

What were we to do? Unlike Geronimo, I don't have access to a time machine. No Speedrat, no Catjet, not even a second-hand TARDIS or a DeLorean. So, zipping back to the future to bring those future GERONIMO STILTON graphic novels to the present isn't going to happen.

But we did come up with a wonderful solution! (I told you we'd have a big announcement coming in this graphic novel!) We've hired two of Geronimo Stilton's favorite writers, Leonardo Favia and Francesco Savino, to continue doing what they've been doing all along—taking Geronimo's stories and turning them into comics. Our translator Nanette McGuinness translates those scripts into English, and editor Carol Burrell passes the edited scripts to artist Ryan Jampole. And Presto! We have all-new, never seen anywhere else on Earth GERONIMO STILTON graphic novels! We never could've done this without the help of our good friends at Atlantyca, the wonderful folks who keep a close eye on everything featuring GERONIMO STILTON, to assure that it meets Geronimo's high standards of excellence. Gee, with Leonardo and Francesco working in Italy, and Nanette, Carol, and Ryan (as well as the letterers and colorists) working in the USA and Canada, this has become quite an international enterprise.

But that's not all! As you can tell by the cover of this very graphic novel, we're also updating our covers to look more like the new GEROMINO STILTON books coming out from our good friends at Scholastic.

Wait! There's still more! The same team we've assembled to do all-new GERONIMO STILTON graphic novels is also creating all-new THEA STILTON graphic novels as well! Just take a look on the following pages and check out the special preview of THEA STILTON #5 "The Secret of the Waterfall in the Woods." And don't forget to look for GERONIMO STILTON #18, coming soon to booksellers everywhere! Geronimo Stilton and his crew continue to save the future, by protecting the past!

See you in the future!

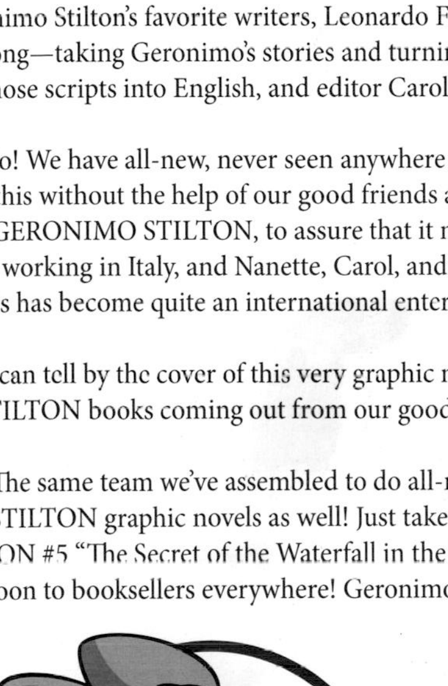

STAY IN TOUCH!

EMAIL: salicrup@papercutz.com
WEB: papercutz.com
TWITTER: @papercutzgn
FACEBOOK: PAPERCUTZGRAPHICNOVELS
FAN MAIL: Papercutz, 160 Broadway, Suite 700, East Wing, New York, NY 10038

Special Preview of THEA STILTON Graphic Novel #5 "The Secret of the Waterfall in the Woods"

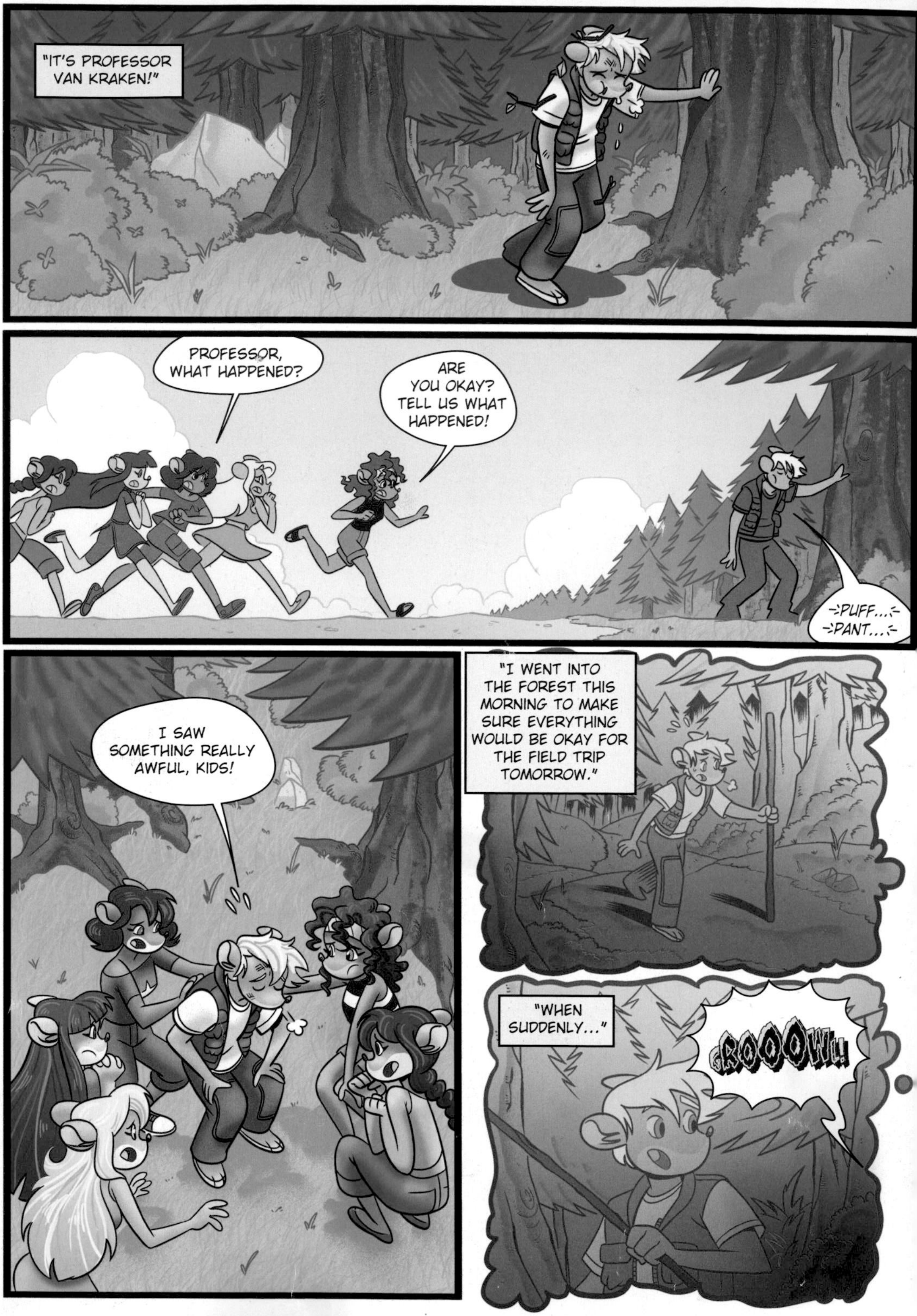
"IT'S PROFESSOR VAN KRAKEN!"
PROFESSOR, WHAT HAPPENED?
ARE YOU OKAY? TELL US WHAT HAPPENED!
PUFF... PANT...
I SAW SOMETHING REALLY AWFUL, KIDS!
"I WENT INTO THE FOREST THIS MORNING TO MAKE SURE EVERYTHING WOULD BE OKAY FOR THE FIELD TRIP TOMORROW."
"WHEN SUDDENLY..."
GROOOWL!

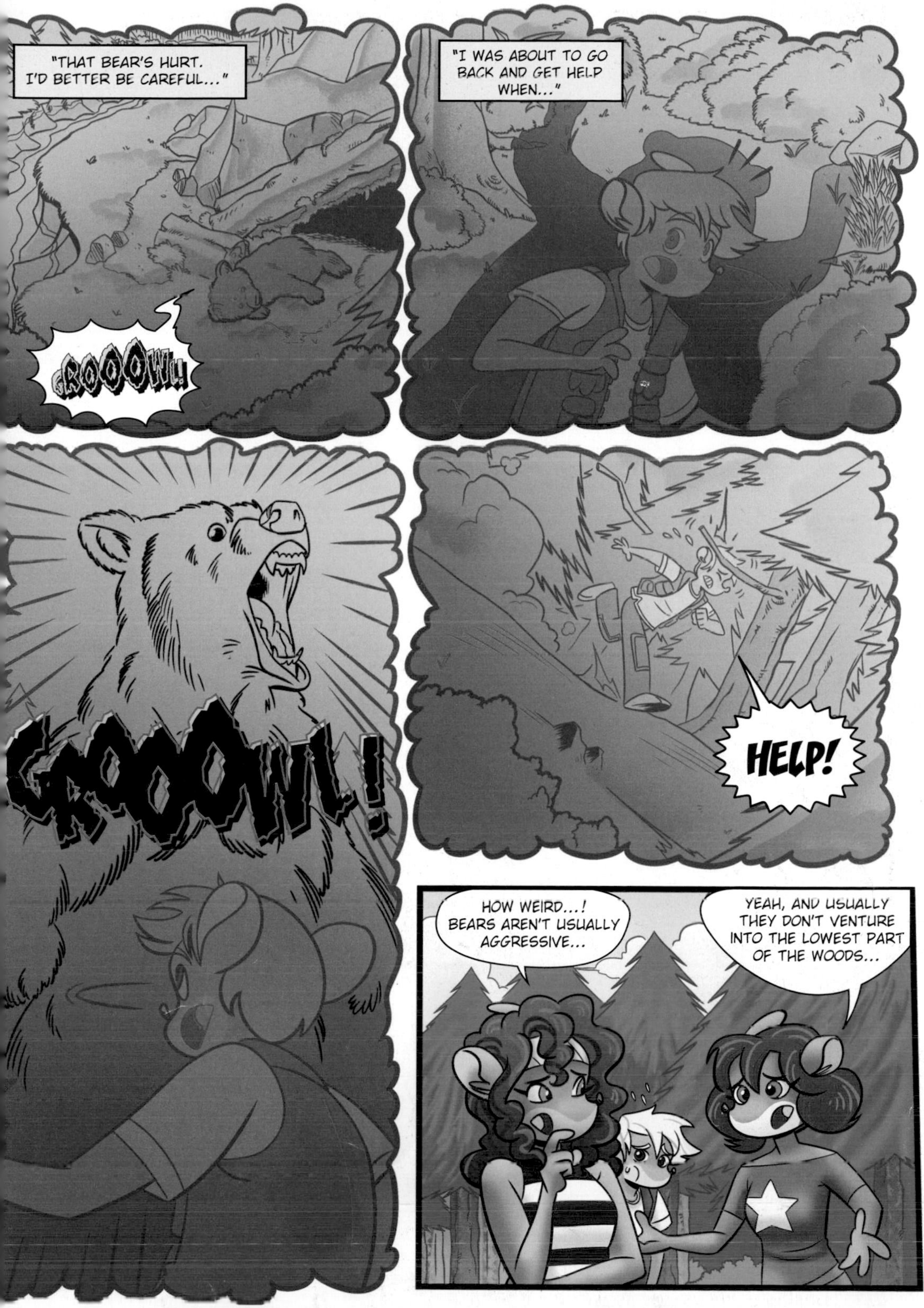
"THAT BEAR'S HURT. I'D BETTER BE CAREFUL..."
GROOOWL!
"I WAS ABOUT TO GO BACK AND GET HELP WHEN..."
GROOOWL!
HELP!
HOW WEIRD...! BEARS AREN'T USUALLY AGGRESSIVE...
YEAH, AND USUALLY THEY DON'T VENTURE INTO THE LOWEST PART OF THE WOODS...

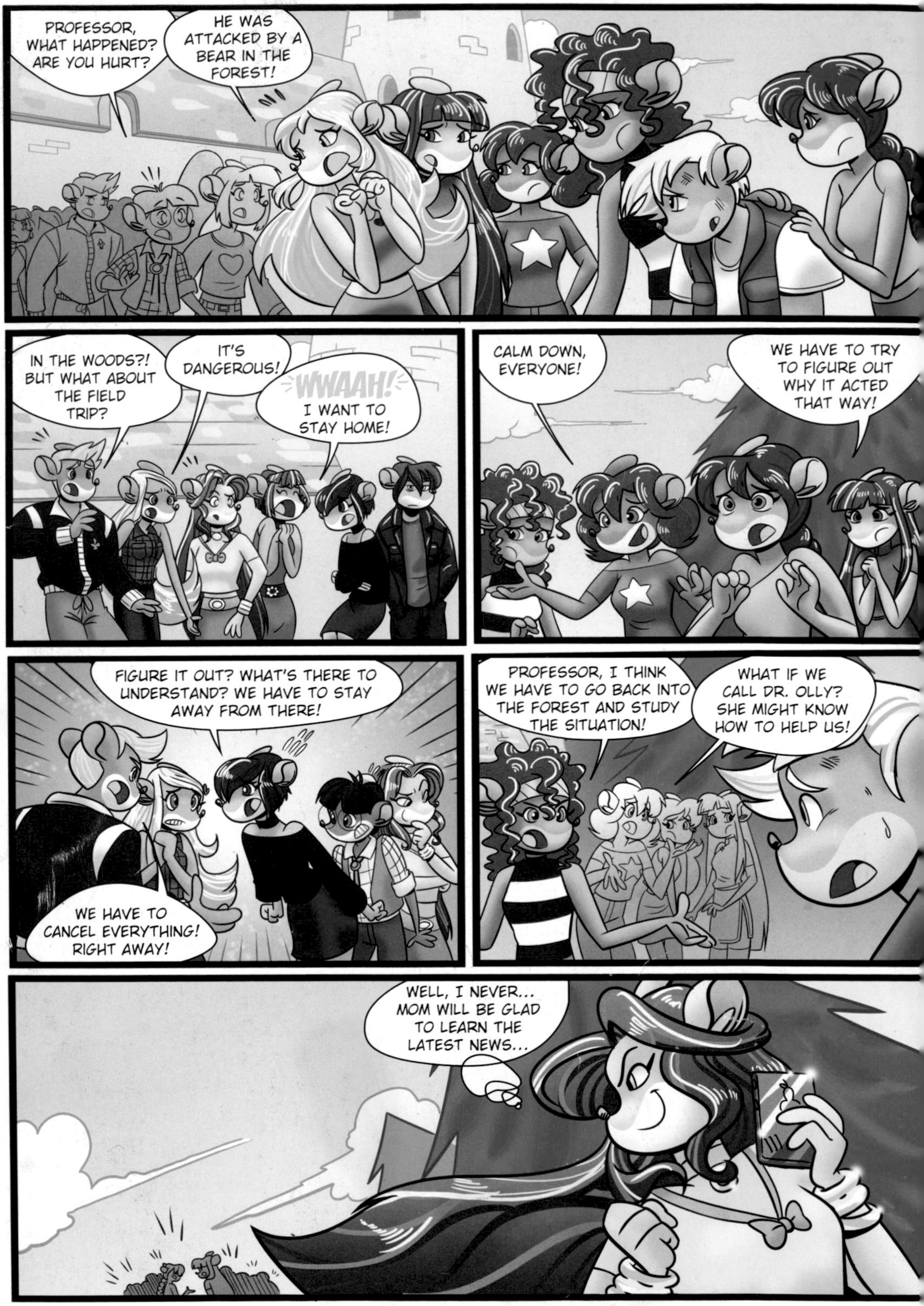
PROFESSOR, WHAT HAPPENED? ARE YOU HURT?
HE WAS ATTACKED BY A BEAR IN THE FOREST!
IN THE WOODS?! BUT WHAT ABOUT THE FIELD TRIP?
IT'S DANGEROUS!
WWAAH! I WANT TO STAY HOME!
CALM DOWN, EVERYONE!
WE HAVE TO TRY TO FIGURE OUT WHY IT ACTED THAT WAY!
FIGURE IT OUT? WHAT'S THERE TO UNDERSTAND? WE HAVE TO STAY AWAY FROM THERE!
WE HAVE TO CANCEL EVERYTHING! RIGHT AWAY!
PROFESSOR, I THINK WE HAVE TO GO BACK INTO THE FOREST AND STUDY THE SITUATION!
WHAT IF WE CALL DR. OLLY? SHE MIGHT KNOW HOW TO HELP US!
WELL, I NEVER... MOM WILL BE GLAD TO LEARN THE LATEST NEWS...

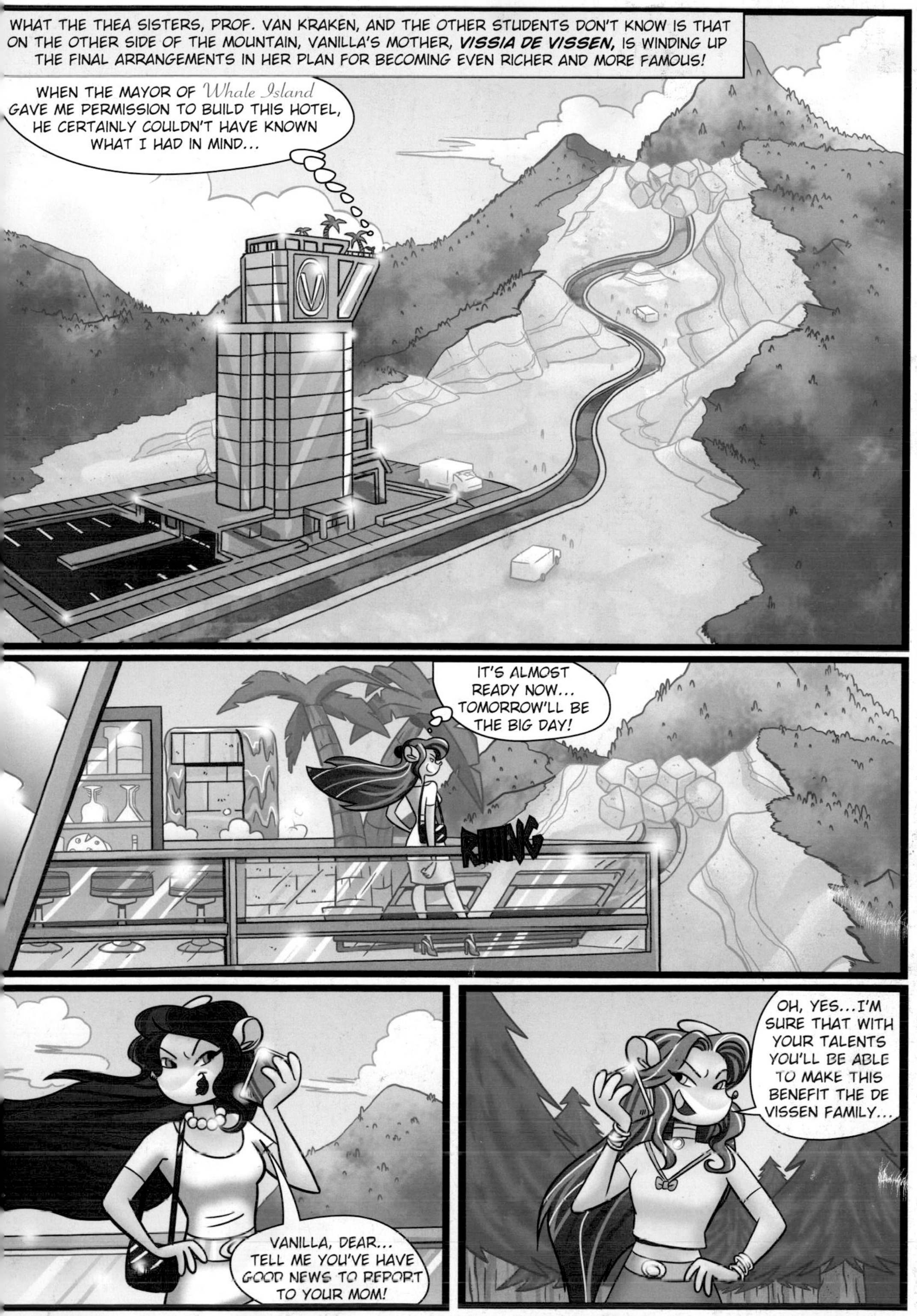
WHAT THE THEA SISTERS, PROF. VAN KRAKEN, AND THE OTHER STUDENTS DON'T KNOW IS THAT ON THE OTHER SIDE OF THE MOUNTAIN, VANILLA'S MOTHER, VISSIA DE VISSEN, IS WINDING UP THE FINAL ARRANGEMENTS IN HER PLAN FOR BECOMING EVEN RICHER AND MORE FAMOUS!
WHEN THE MAYOR OF Whale Island GAVE ME PERMISSION TO BUILD THIS HOTEL, HE CERTAINLY COULDN'T HAVE KNOWN WHAT I HAD IN MIND...
IT'S ALMOST READY NOW... TOMORROW'LL BE THE BIG DAY!
RIIIING
VANILLA, DEAR... TELL ME YOU'VE HAVE GOOD NEWS TO REPORT TO YOUR MOM!
OH, YES...I'M SURE THAT WITH YOUR TALENTS YOU'LL BE ABLE TO MAKE THIS BENEFIT THE DE VISSEN FAMILY...

Don't Miss THEA STILTON Graphic Novel #5 "The Secret of the Waterfall in the Woods"!

Geronimo Stilton boxed sets!
Three Graphic Novels collected in each box!

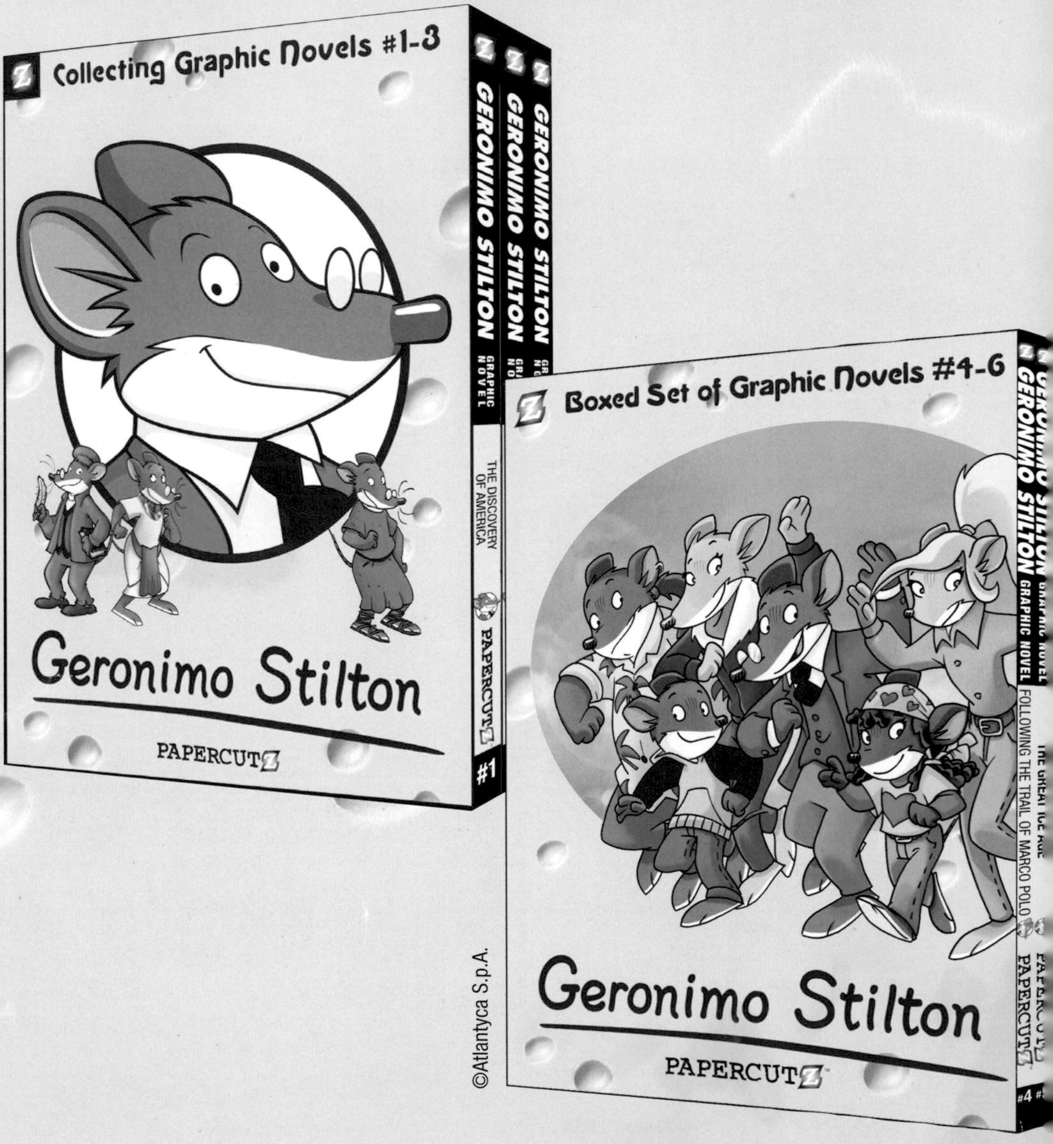
Collecting Graphic Novels #1-3
Geronimo Stilton
PAPERCUTZ
GERONIMO STILTON
GRAPHIC NOVEL
THE DISCOVERY OF AMERICA
PAPERCUTZ
#1
Boxed Set of Graphic Novels #4-6
Geronimo Stilton
PAPERCUTZ
GERONIMO STILTON
GRAPHIC NOVEL
FOLLOWING THE TRAIL OF MARCO POLO
PAPERCUTZ
#4

Available at booksellers everywhere.

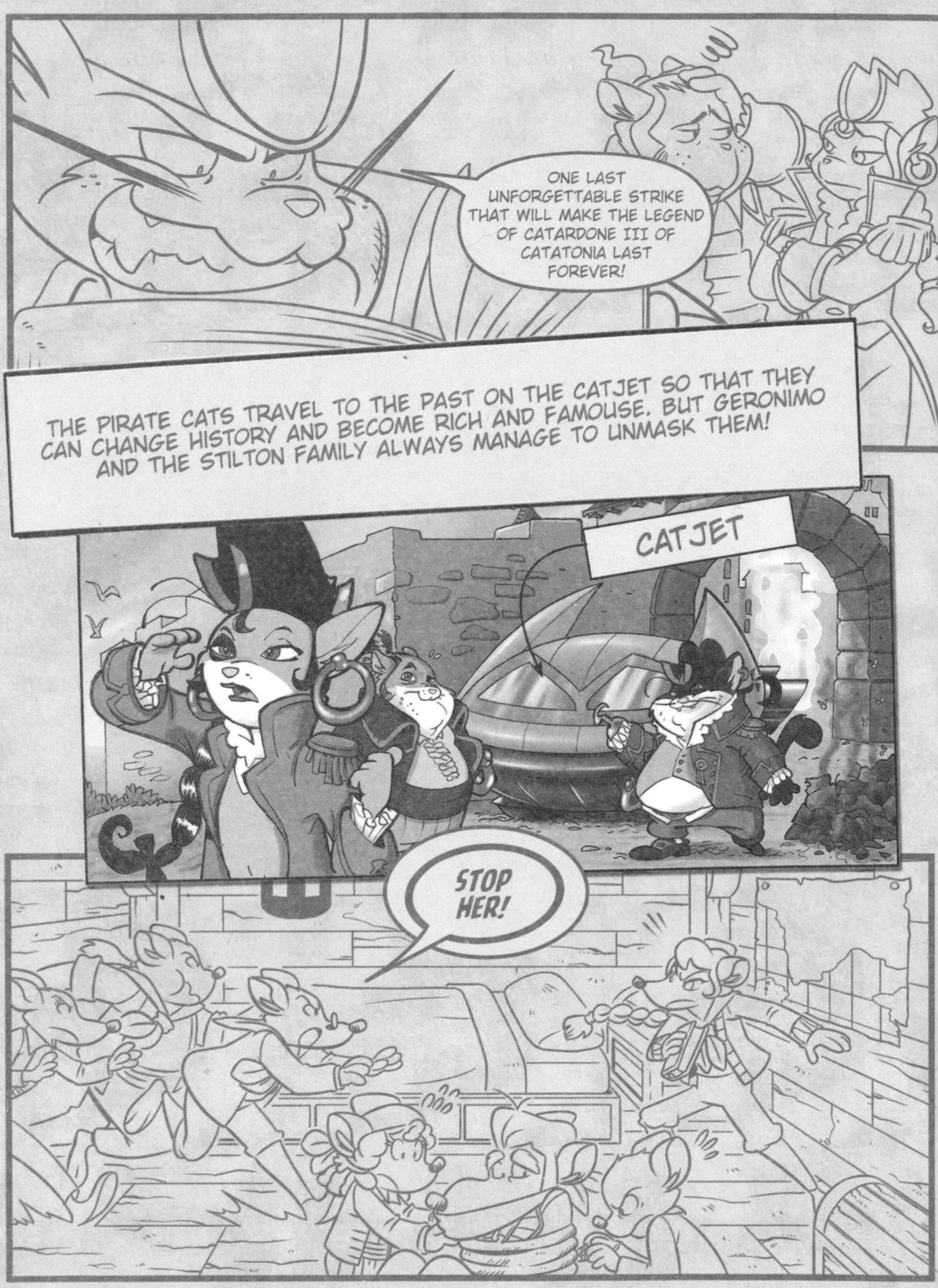
ONE LAST UNFORGETTABLE STRIKE THAT WILL MAKE THE LEGEND OF CATARDONE III OF CATATONIA LAST FOREVER!
THE PIRATE CATS TRAVEL TO THE PAST ON THE CATJET SO THAT THEY CAN CHANGE HISTORY AND BECOME RICH AND FAMOUSE. BUT GERONIMO AND THE STILTON FAMILY ALWAYS MANAGE TO UNMASK THEM!
CATJET
STOP HER!